BETWIXT and Bewitched

A Woody Lake Mystery
Book #2

Rennae Todd

Jakada Books
PERTH, WESTERN AUSTRALIA

Betwixt and Bewitched: Rennae Todd / Jakada Books / Perth Western Australia

D2D edition ISBN: 978-0-6454212-7-9

In this Story

Betwixt and Bewitched is the second title in the Woody Lake Mystery series set in the fictional outer-Perth suburbs of Woody Lake and Rosny, located on either side of the Cygnet River.

In this story, Hettie Parke is still President of the Parke Croquet Club, and daughter Violet still runs the Club Cafe. The story opens with a croquet game, but life is about to get complicated very quickly, and it isn't something Hettie can solve with a croquet mallet. Aunt Alice finds herself in trouble, there's a shoplifting spree that's baffling police, and something is upsetting Ceefer.

Main Characters

<u>Parke Family</u>

Henrietta (Hettie) Parke: (48) Relief teacher, president of the Parke Croquet. Divorced from Brian Hitchcock (deceased). Lives at 6 Old Dairy Road.

Ceefer: a black cat recently arrived in Hettie's life. Has talents not yet fully understood.

Violet Hitchcock: Hettie's daughter (22). Runs the Club Cafe. Lives with Hettie.

Elly and Rafe Figeroa: Hettie's daughter (27), works part-time in advertising. Married to landscape designer Rafe. Two daughters, Jazmin (4) and Rosa (2). Live at 4 Old Dairy Road.

Jack and California (Callie) Parke: Hettie's parents. Live in a villa unit at Sunny Vale Retirement Village.

Alice and Roscoe Slater: Alice is Jack's Parke's younger sister, married to retired antique dealer Roscoe. Live at 8 Old Dairy Road.

Larry and Gwen Parke: Hettie's brother (46). Plays bowls. They run Parke Real Estate Agency. Live at 2 Old Dairy Road.

Pearl, Max and Maxxie Longchamp: Hettie's younger sister (37). Married to businessman Max. Son Maxxie (20) is a university student. Live on Rosny Circle.

Eddie, Gloria and Frank Garcia: Related to Callie Parke. Eddie is a retired plumber. Son Frank is a primary school sports teacher. Eddie's sister Gloria favours conspiracy theories. They occupy two houses further along Old Dairy Road.

Croquet Club Members

Judy Sanford: nurse, Hettie's friend.

Romola Asquith: Club Secretary, wife & mother, Hettie's friend.

Belle Danvers: ghostwriter, Hettie's friend .

Andrew Asquith: accountant, Club treasurer, Romola's brother-in-law.

Tom Eastbourne: Club captain

Len Travers: a useful man.

Bowls Club Members

George Engles: President.

Gary Asquith: Romola's husband, owns a small airline charter business.

Sandra Alberts: Committee member, dog Brutus.

Others

Detective Inspector Grayson Fox: Homicide squad. Someone Hettie used to know.

Sergeant Stuart Higgins: In charge of Rosny Police Station.

Dan Wallace: reporter for the *Rosny Record*.

Mrs. Edith Braxton and Mrs. Ila Bronson: known as the Mrs. B's. They frequent the Club Cafe and live opposite on Old Dairy Road.

Janelle Rice: knew Ceefer's previous owner, Miranda. Has a white Persian named Aurora who is Ceefer's troublesome friend.

Lil Walters: tenant at 10 Old Dairy Road, dog Howie.

Henry & Lucy Dunlop: neighbours at 8 Daisy Street.

Parke Trust

Bladen (Den) Barrett: former mayor of Cygnet LGA.

Isolde Reflex: lawyer.

Darla Dalrymple: owner of Top Cut Hair Salons.

Chapter 1

"Seven-five," Jo Isaacs announced as her partner Susie Merritt casually tapped her blue ball through the twelfth hoop for the win. "Good game," she added with a glint of triumph as the two women shook hands with Hettie Parke and Judy Sanford.

Hettie tried not to glare at the Isaacs woman. She was looking far too pleased with herself. Winning was one thing, gloating about it quite another.

"I need a coffee," Hettie said, as they put their mallets in the rack by the clubroom door. One group of croquet players were already sitting out on the patio with coffee and biscuits. Hettie's group went to the kitchen, via the croquet clubroom.

"Hello, George," Hettie greeted George Engles, president of the Bowls Club, who was stirring milk into his cup of anaemic looking tea at the kitchen bench. "How are things?"

The bowls and croquet players didn't see as much of one another as they used to when they shared the one space. The Bowls Club had recently taken over the new clubroom at the back of the Clubhouse leaving the original clubroom for the exclusive use of the Croquet Club. Hettie found it to be a mixed blessing. Their room didn't feel as vibrant. She expected she would get used to it.

"Good, good," George said now. "Fiona will be back home on Tuesday." A huge smile split his pleasant, square-jawed face.

"That is good news. I'm so glad for you all," Hettie said, her congratulations echoed by other players in the kitchen. George's daughter battled a drug addiction and had spent the past six months in a private rehab facility. It had cost her family dearly but, by all accounts, she had done well.

"Thank you," George replied. He lowered his voice. "Do you have a moment, Hettie?"

"Yes, sure." Hettie made her coffee and followed George into the bowls clubroom. "What is it?" she asked when George seemed a little hesitant to speak.

"Ah, I was just wondering how you were getting on with that plan of yours. You know, to increase the number of croquet courts."

"I'm still waiting on the Trustees to make a decision."

The Clubs occupied part of the parkland

managed by the Parke Trust. The Trustees were not known for making prompt decisions when it came to change, and Hettie was asking for more land for the Croquet Club.

"I suppose Jack is backing you," George said. Hettie thought she heard some bitterness there.

"I really don't know," she told him. She didn't. Her father hadn't commented either way when she'd told him what she wanted, though he would have the final say if the Trustees were tied on a decision. Hettie expected he would probably back her request in the end, unless the Trustees were completely against it. Jack Parke was nothing if not judicious.

"It won't change anything, George," she assured him. "We each have our own space now."

"I suppose."

Hettie sighed as George went out to join his fellow Bowls Club members on the patio on the other side of the Clubhouse. That paranoia about her wanting to take over the Clubhouse was still doing the rounds it seemed.

An hour later, all equipment trolleys safely stowed, and lights turned off, Hettie saw the last player out before locking the patio doors. At the top end of the clubroom, she went through the private entrance into the back of the Club Cafe, intending to check in on Violet, before she went home. The Cafe would be open until five.

"Merrrooow," Ceefer greeted her as she entered the seating area, deserting his usual post at the central table occupied by the Mrs. B's. That cat knew where he would get the most handouts.

"What's the matter?" Hettie asked him as she bent to rub his furry black head. She had barely finished speaking when an ambulance, siren wailing, sped past the building. Customers craned their necks to see where it was going. Violet, and her assistant Tess, both came out of the kitchen. The ambulance rounded the bend at the end of the park and drew to a halt.

Mrs. Braxton had pushed back her chair and was half standing. "Hettie, has it stopped at your house?"

Hettie approached the side window and stared down the park. "I think it's next door."

"Alice?" said Mrs. Bronson, her forehead creased with concern. The elderly Mrs. B's were friends of Hettie's Aunt Alice, all being in their seventies and living in Old Dairy Road.

"You'd best run and see, dear," Mrs. Braxton said.

"I'm coming too." Violet pulled off her apron and tossed it to Tess.

Hettie glanced at her daughter and then at the customers in the Cafe. The place was full of the lunchtime crowd.

"Of course, you must," Mrs. Bronson told them. "We'll hold the fort here with Tess. Off you go."

Hettie tried not to think about what they might find as they ran down the park, Violet outstripping her with every stride. As she got closer, she could see Aunt Alice standing in the front garden and felt she could breathe again. Elly was there too, her arm around her aunt. Violet dashed across the Road, but Hettie was forced to wait as a car drove by. It was a good excuse to catch her breath before crossing the Road.

Lil Walters, the neighbour on the other side of Aunt Alice's house, was standing with them. Her dog, Howie, a large animal of indeterminate breed, was lying, panting, at her feet. Lil stepped back as Hettie came up and gave her aunt a hug.

"What's happening?"

"He fell off the ladder," Alice whispered.

"Uncle Roscoe? Is he alright?"

"He's dead, Hettie. He broke his neck," Aunt Alice whispered. Violet gasped and

Hettie reached for her hand.

"Are you sure?"

"He hit the edge of the wheelbarrow."

The front door opened, and an ambulance officer came out of the house and approached them. "We need to wait for the police," he said. "They're on their way."

"The police?" Hettie all but squeaked.

"It's standard procedure for an accidental death," the officer replied. "We can't interfere with the scene until the police have viewed it and given clearance."

"Oh, right." Hettie decided it didn't need all of them waiting outside for the police. "Girls, why don't you take Aunt Alice inside and make her a cup of tea." She gave her aunt another hug and watched the three of them disappear inside.

"Apparently he was cleaning the gutters," Lil said sotto voce. "He probably had a heart attack."

"It's certainly possible. He'd just had his seventy-eighth birthday, after all." Lil nodded. "Did you hear the ambulance?" Hettie asked her.

"No. I found Alice out here when I came back from walking Howie."

"Oh, thank you for waiting with her, Lil. It must have been a great shock for her."

Lil Walters was a tall woman with a pleasant round face, and short brown hair worn with a fringe that met the top of her dark-rimmed glasses. Hettie hadn't had much to do with her since she'd moved into Max and Pearl's old house several months earlier, but her first impression of the woman as the calm, competent sort seemed to have been born out. A police car turned into Old Dairy Road.

"I'll leave you to it then," Lil said. "Tell Alice I'll call in on her tomorrow. Come along, Howie."

"I will, and thanks again."

The police car pulled up and Sergeant Stuart Higgins from the Rosny Police Station got out. He was a solidly built man in his forties, just meeting regulation height, which meant three inches taller than Hettie's five-foot-seven.

"Hello Stuart."

"Hettie. I received a report of a possible accidental death. Not a family member, I hope?"

"My aunt's husband, Roscoe Slater."

Stuart nodded. "My condolences. I need to take a look at the scene."

"Of course."

The ambulance officer led Stuart into the house, and Hettie followed, entering the living room as the men continued out through the back door.

Aunt Alice was sitting on the sofa, cup of tea in hand and biscuits on the coffee table. Elly and Violet were on either side of her, Elly with an arm around her aunt's shoulder and Violet holding her free hand. A metallic tap, tapping was coming from nearby. Hettie went into the kitchen, curious to know what the sound was, but also to get a look at the scene outside.

A strip of guttering swung loose, tapping against the kitchen window. Moving closer to the window she caught sight of the wheelbarrow, half full of dead leaves. And Roscoe with his head hanging over the side like a puppet when the string was let go. She gulped and turned away. He must have made a grab for the gutter to save himself from falling and it had come away from the roof.

Hettie went back to the living room. Elly was texting on her phone. "I'm just letting Rafe know," she said.

"You'll come stay with us for the next few days," Hettie told Aunt Alice.

"What? Oh, no, I'll be fine here, Hettie," Aunt Alice replied. "There's no need to fuss."

It was clear Aunt Alice was not fine. She seemed in a daze, staring into space but not seeing anything. Unless it was Uncle Roscoe with his head in the wheelbarrow. She was in shock. Aunt Alice never wanted to be a burden on anyone but right now she needed to let herself be looked after.

"Then one of us will stay with you. You shouldn't be on your own just now."

"Well…"

"I'll come and sleep over at your house," Violet offered.

"Oh, dear, it's very thoughtful of you," Aunt Alice said. "If you're sure. I don't want to put you out, but I wouldn't want to leave my cats on their own at night."

Hettie wasn't sure they would notice so long as their bowls were full, but of course she wouldn't say so.

"You'll come and spend the day at my place now, anyway. No argument about that, Auntie. I'll call Pop and everyone and let them know what's happened. They'll want to visit."

Violet left for the Cafe shortly after, concerned at how Tess and the Mrs. B's were managing. Hettie took her place on the sofa beside Aunt Alice. Elly made another pot of tea and a coffee for her mother. Stuart Higgins came in to talk to them. He shook his head at the offer of a drink and sat with his notebook. Hettie caught movement outside on the street and saw the ambulance officers loading the gurney into the back of the vehicle. It left quietly.

"I just need to get some details from you, Mrs. Slater," Stuart said. "Can you tell me what happened?"

"I don't know. I was vacuuming the floors," Aunt Alice replied, her voice breaking on the last word. Hettie squeezed her hand and heard Aunt Alice take a deep breath and steady herself. "I didn't hear anything over the noise of the vacuum cleaner. The first I knew that something was wrong was when I got to the dining room, and I saw something moving outside the kitchen window. I went to look and saw the gutter hanging and then I saw Roscoe. He was lying on the wheelbarrow, and the ladder was on the ground."

"Was anyone in the backyard at the time?" Stuart asked.

Aunt Alice looked at him, a little puzzled. "No one else lives here. There's just the… two of us," she added her voice falling away.

"Did you have any visitors this morning?" Aunt Alice shook her head. "Is the small gate at the front always locked?"

"Yes, it is."

"Always?"

"Yes. It can only be opened from inside

and the bolt is too low down to reach from outside. Oh, of all the stupid things," she said suddenly, her voice rising, frustration and anger evident. "He was too old to be up on ladders cleaning gutters. I told him so. I should have known better. I should have told him to go ahead; we need to scrimp and save every penny. He would have paid someone to do it then just to prove me wrong." Her voice broke on the last words.

"You can't blame yourself," Elly cried.

Stuart closed his notebook. "I'll leave it at that for now, Mrs. Slater. We'll see what the autopsy has to say."

"An autopsy?" Hettie asked.

"It's normal procedure in the circumstances. There may be an underlying reason for Mr. Slater to have fallen."

"Like a heart attack?" Stuart nodded.

After he'd left, Hettie called her father and Larry to let them know what had happened. Larry said he'd pass the message to Eddie and Pearl. Before she and Aunt Alice went across to her house Hettie checked that all was well. Snuggly and Puggsy's bowls were full, their water topped up, all lights were off, and nothing was turned on in the kitchen. So why did she have the niggling feeling she was missing something?

Chapter 2

Jack Parke pulled his sister into an awkward hug. Awkward because of his back problem and the cane he used, but also because he wasn't a demonstrative man.

Aunt Alice patted his shoulder. Jack's wife Callie, dressed fashionably in funereal black which contrasted dramatically with her blonde, blue-eyed colouring, dispensed air kisses and murmured condolences that barely even sounded sincere. The sisters-in-law had never gotten along.

"Sit down, Jack," Aunt Alice said taking her seat again on the sofa in Hettie's living room and indicating an armchair. Callie joined her on the sofa a little distance apart, but not before checking for cat hair.

Hettie offered tea and coffee and went into the kitchen to make the drinks. There were iced strawberry cupcakes too, run over from the Cafe by Tess.

Hettie heard Jack telling Aunt Alice he would deal with the funeral arrangements.

"There's no need for you to do anything," he said.

"Thank you, Jack. Can he be buried in the old cemetery?"

"Is that what you want?"

The old cemetery, that parched piece of land where the early white settlers in the area had been buried, was now part of the land holdings managed by the Parke Trust. The last time Hettie had been there was when her grandmother, Florrie Parke, had been put to rest some years ago. Florrie had only outlived her husband by a few months.

The development agreement for Terry Parke's Sunny Vale Dairy Farm allowed the next generation of Parkes the choice of joining their ancestors in the old cemetery.

"I would like that, seeing as Alan is already buried there," Alice said after a moment, referring to her first husband. "I'll be there myself eventually."

Jack nodded. "All right. We can do that. You're not to worry about anything, you understand. You're in good shape financially."

Alice just nodded. There was no need to elaborate. The family knew Jack had squirrelled away the money she'd received for the sale of her house when she married Roscoe Slater. He hadn't trusted the man with his sister's funds.

Knowing her father, Hettie was sure it had been invested wisely.

"This is a good time for you to consider moving into the Sunny Vale Nursing Home, Alice dear," Callie said brightly, eyeing the cupcakes but not taking one.

Aunt Alice's eyes widened. "The Nursing Home, California?" she queried. "I'm younger than you and I haven't even made it to a Sunny Vale villa yet. I imagine you'll get to the Nursing Home long before I do."

Callie gave a brittle laugh. "Oh, that's hardly likely." If she had more to add they weren't to hear it. Jack cleared his throat and Callie subsided.

"That policeman, Sergeant Higgins, said there's to be an autopsy," Aunt Alice said. "I don't know how these things work, Jack. The hospital took care of all that when Alan died."

Jack looked a little bemused. "Is there any reason to suppose Roscoe didn't die from falling off his ladder?"

"No. At least… except he might have had a heart attack."

"That's possible. You didn't move him, did you? Before the ambulance officers or the police arrived?" Aunt Alice shook her head. "Well, there's no need for you to concern yourself with any of that, Allie," Jack said gruffly. "It's just routine."

Hettie reached for a cupcake, as much for something to do as anything. She heard the back door open, and Larry came in through the kitchen. He greeted everyone and went to give Aunt Alice a hug.

"I'm sorry Gwen can't be here right now, Aunt Alice, but she'll be along later. She's managing Home Opens today."

"It's good of you to come, Larry."

Callie had him sit beside her, although it was Jack he conversed with for the most part. Conversation, as was usually the case at times like these, was stilted.

When the parents eventually made to leave Larry helped Jack to his feet and walked them out to where his gopher was waiting in the driveway. Aunt Alice closed her eyes.

"Would you like to have a rest," Hettie asked. "You're welcome to use Elly's room anytime, you know that." Elly hadn't lived at home for almost six years but the bedroom that was now the spare room was still referred to as hers.

"I think I will, thank you." Aunt Alice rubbed her forehead. "Would you have something for a headache?"

Hettie did and soon had Aunt Alice comfortably settled. Larry came back in, and they had another cup of coffee and helped themselves to the cupcakes.

"Where did you get to this morning?" Hettie asked him.

"I had a Home Open to deal with at twelve, so I left the Club early. Then I had to call on Steph to take over my two o'clock after you rang," Larry said, referring to one of his agents. "It's a bit mad out there right now, with houses coming on the market."

Hettie wondered if a murder on her croquet courts several months ago had anything to do with that. At least Uncle Roscoe's death wasn't murder. She couldn't help wondering if Aunt Alice's life would be freer now, once she had gotten through her grief. Roscoe Slater hadn't been the most pleasant of men since he'd lost his antique shop and found himself living in Woody Lake.

"**I** was just checking on Alice but she's not home," Lil Walters said when Hettie opened her front door mid-afternoon next day, in answer to her doorbell.

"She's here," Hettie said. "Come on in. We're just having afternoon tea."

"Oh, I don't want to intrude."

"You're not. Please, come in and join the

gang."

"Ah, I see what you mean," Lil said as they entered the living room. Hettie dodged her granddaughters as she crossed to the dining room. Elly's little girls were on the floor entertaining Ceefer, or vice versa. Rafe, coffee cup in hand watched over them from the sofa, seated beside Pearl's husband, Max, and Frank Garcia.

Gathered around the dining table were Elly, Violet, Maxxie, Pearl, Aunt Alice, the Mrs. B's, and Gloria and Eddie Garcia. Lil had already met Violet and Elly, but hadn't met the Mrs. B's, although she'd seen them at the Cafe, and was on nodding acquaintance with the Garcia brother and sister who occupied the two houses on the other side of the vacant lot next to her house.

"The Garcias are my mother's relations," Hettie explained. "She was a Garcia before she married. And Frank over there, next to my son-in-law, Rafe, is Eddie's son. I think that makes him my second cousin once removed."

Frank waved a greeting. "Don't stress over it," he said to Lil. "We have enough trouble keeping everything straight ourselves."

"I didn't realise you were all related," Lil said. "It must be nice having so much family nearby."

"Most of the time," Eddie told her.

This was greeted with some quiet laughter, subdued due to the circumstances of their gathering.

"Will you have a coffee, or tea?" Hettie asked, as Eddie pulled out a chair for Lil.

"Coffee, thanks, Hettie," she said, sitting. "How have you been Alice? I'm not sure I will be able to get up on a ladder again for some time myself. Do you think poor Roscoe may have had a heart attack?"

"It's possible. There's to be an autopsy." Lil nodded.

"He was probably startled by a drone flying overhead," Gloria said. "I've seen a few around lately. It's the government, you know. Spying on us."

Gloria's comment startled Lil, but no one else was surprised or made any comment. Hettie put a coffee in front of Lil and sat down again. Elly passed around the plate of fudge brownies and then took the few remaining over to the boys who were now arguing about Aussie Rules' football. Nothing new there. They supported different State teams.

"Gloria and I are going on a wine cruise on the Swan River Thursday week," Eddie said to Aunt Alice. "Why don't you come along with us?"

"Oh, I don't know, Eddie."

"You mustn't sit around and mope. Let me know by Tuesday, yeah? What about you Hettie?"

"I'm still teaching at Rosny Primary, Eddie. I've another three weeks to go."

"I did tell you that, Dad," Frank said in the background. Frank knew what Hettie was doing because he was the sports teacher at the school.

"You tell me lots of things," Eddie replied.

"Why don't we go, Ila?" Mrs. Braxton said eagerly to Mrs. Bronson. "It's ages since we took a nice cruise on the river. And a visit to a winery."

Mrs. Bronson shook her head in amusement. "We can visit a winery any time. They're only a few miles over."

"It's not the same. Think of cruising down the Swan, the birds on the water, the sun shining. Besides, we'll be in nice company." Mrs. Braxton stole a quick glance at Gloria, who was rolling her cup around, studying the tea leaves.

"I'd enjoy the company," Eddie said, looking at them almost pleadingly. Hettie knew he did his best for his sister but dealing with her conspiracy theories could get tiring. At least they didn't live together.

"Let's do that then," Mrs. Bronson agreed.

"What about you, Lil?" Eddie asked. "The more the merrier."

Lil looked at Alice and shook her head. "Thanks, but no, Eddie. Another time perhaps. Thank you for the coffee, Hettie," she said getting to her feet, "and lovely to meet you all, but I must get on. I just wanted to pop in and say hello to Alice."

Hettie saw her out. "Did Sergeant Higgins speak to you yesterday?" she asked Lil, as they lingered on the front porch.

"He did. I couldn't help him though. I was out walking Howie. It was so nice out. I wasn't in a hurry to get home."

"It's only someone at your house or mine who might have heard anything," Hettie said. "Or perhaps someone at the back if they were out in their yard."

Lil nodded. "I was on my way home when I saw Alice out front. She looked upset so I spoke to her. She didn't have a phone, so I called the ambulance."

"You called the ambulance?"

"I did. Alice didn't seem to know what she was about. I couldn't make sense of what she was saying at first, so I went into the backyard to see for myself. That's when I called the ambulance. But he was already gone. I could see that. Terrible thing to happen."

"I didn't know that, Lil. Thank goodness you were there. Did you see anyone else in the street when you were coming home?"

"No one suspicious looking, if that's what you mean. Is there a problem? You're not with the police, are you? I thought you said you were teaching."

"I am, as a relief teacher. But there are always questions when someone dies accidentally. Especially when there are no witnesses."

"I guess so. I think they'll find he had a heart attack, or perhaps he just lost his balance." Hettie agreed. "I'll check in on Alice occasionally while you're working, Hettie. Don't worry about her."

"That's very thoughtful of you, Lil." She was left wondering why Aunt Alice hadn't called the ambulance herself.

Violet slept over at her aunt's house again on Monday night, as she had done the two nights previous, but on Tuesday evening, Aunt Alice didn't answer when Violet knocked on her back door.

"She's probably just gone to bed early, Vi," Hettie reasoned, when Violet came back and told her. "I'll check on her in the morning. You know how she doesn't like to be fussed over."

"I guess."

But it did puzzle Hettie that Aunt Alice hadn't told them if she didn't want Violet to sleep over anymore. She hoped her aunt wasn't going into a depression, so she was relieved to see her watering her roses when she opened her garage door next morning.

"Oh, yes, well, I was spring cleaning, and I was tired, so I went to bed early. I guess I didn't hear Vi knock," Aunt Alice explained when Hettie asked her about it

"She would have been upset anyway, if she'd woken you," Hettie said.

"It's lovely of her, but I really don't need her to keep coming over, Hettie. Sometimes I do just want to go to bed early. Far too early for a young thing like Violet."

"Whatever you want, Aunt Alice. We just want to be sure you're okay.

"I am dear. I just need some time to myself for now. Have a nice day at school."

As Hettie drove out, she turned to wave, but Aunt Alice was looking over her shoulder at something and didn't notice.

Chapter 3

Hettie forgot all about it as she dealt with the Grade Five class at Rosny Primary. She was already looking forward to her six-week stint of teaching to be over. It had been some time since she'd worked for longer than a week or two at a time. Usually it was only a matter of a day or three.

She and Frank found they were both on playground duty at lunchtime. Frank was munching an apple as he wandered down toward the sports ground where a casual game of football was in progress. It didn't take long before it turned into a coaching session leaving Hettie supervising the rest of the playground alone. It didn't surprise her. Frank was sports mad, and a good teacher as well she had to admit. An idea began to form in her mind.

As they made their way back into the school building after the lunch break, Hettie asked him if he'd ever considered joining the Bowls Club or the Croquet Club.

"In another thirty years maybe," he said.

"They're not old-people's games, Frank," she said. "Most of the top croquet players in the world are in their twenties to forties. You're in that age range. Imagine playing for Australia against Egypt or England for example."

"Desperate for members at your club are you?"

"Not at all, but our club wouldn't mind nurturing someone with the potential to be a top state or national player," she told him.

She hurried off to her classroom before he had a chance to reply. Let him think about it. It would be another feather in the Club's cap if they produced such a player and she considered Frank a good prospect. She didn't know why she hadn't thought of it before this.

She always looked forward to Wednesday night at the Croquet Club, and because she was working right now there was nothing better than having dinner at the Café as well. Tonight she decided she would ask Aunt Alice if she wanted to join her. She put her car in the garage when she got home from school and popped next door to invite her. But there was no answer to her knock. Aunt Alice could be anywhere after all. At the Café, at Elly's place, visiting Jack and Callie, or visiting one of the Mrs. B's, or both.

She decided to call Elly first. If Aunt Alice wasn't there Elly might know where she was.

"Hello love," Hettie said when Elly answered her phone. "Have you seen Aunt Alice today?"

"She's here, Mum," Elly told her. Hettie could hear the television and children's voices in the background.

"I wanted to ask her if she'd like to have dinner at the Café tonight," Hettie said.

"Um, she's asleep."

"Is everything alright?" Hettie asked, sensing something in her daughter's voice that suggested perhaps it wasn't.

"I need to talk to you."

"I'll come over, love," Hettie said, wondering what it was about. Less than a minute later she was knocking on Elly's back door. Hettie didn't always lock her own back door when she was home, but Elly did because of the children.

"Nan," Jazmin cried throwing herself at her grandmother after Elly let her. Hettie hugged her and then Rosa.

"Is Aunt Alice sleeping through all this?" Hettie asked. The television was still on.

Elly nodded. Hettie followed her into the living room. Aunt Alice was fast asleep in an armchair.

"She came over for morning tea," Elly said quietly. "And she's been asleep most of the afternoon. But I'm worried about her Mum. She's behaving very oddly."

"Oh? What has she been doing?" Hettie asked. But before Elly could answer little Rosa was tugging on Aunt Alice's arm.

"Auntie, Auntie, play," she demanded.

Aunt Alice sat up. "Oh, did I drop off?" She looked around, seeming to take a moment to get her bearings. "Hello Hettie. You're home early."

"It's almost four o'clock, Auntie," Hettie said. "I called in to see if you would like to have dinner at the Café tonight?"

"Oh, my goodness. Um, yes, I guess so. That would be nice. Do you think Ila and Edith might be there tonight?"

"Why don't we give them a call and find out? Let's go over to my place now and let Elly get the girls their dinner. We can have a coffee and a chat before we go to the Café."

Aunt Alice nodded. "I need to pay a visit to the bathroom first," she said.

"Play, Auntie," Rosa cried as Aunt Alice got to her feet.

"We'll play later, dear," she told her great-niece and went off down the hall. Elly picked up her daughter and took her into the kitchen.

Hettie followed, leaving Jazmin watching the television.

"So what is the problem?" Hettie asked.

Elly glanced in the general direction of the bathroom. "If I'm only able to tell you the beginning of it before she comes back you'll think I'm nuts," she said. "How about I come over after you and Vi get home tonight."

Hettie was concerned now because it wasn't like Elly to worry over nothing.

"Alright then, we'll see you after nine." She would just have to be patient for a few hours. Aunt Alice returned and they left for Hettie's house.

"The hinges need oiling," Aunt Alice said as Hettie tugged open the gate in the side fence. The hinges were indeed stiff. "I'll get Roscoe…." She stopped, her hand going to her mouth. Hettie put her arm around her aunt's shoulder and they went inside. Roscoe wouldn't be oiling any gate hinges.

After eating dinner with Aunt Alice and the Mrs. B's Hettie joined her club members on the croquet courts while her aunt went across the road with her friends to Ila Bronson's house. There was a movie on television they wanted to watch.

"It's a Judy Dench," Edith Braxton explained over dinner. "I've forgotten how many times we've seen her movies, but we never get tired of them." The three elderly ladies all agreed she was their favourite actress. Hettie was just glad Aunt Alice had company for the evening.

"I'm surprised," Hettie said later as her members sat over coffee and biscuits in the clubroom, "that none of our members have ever made it onto the state team. Do you think that's because they don't want to commit themselves, or aren't up to that level?"

"It is a commitment," Judy said. "You need to attend coaching and practice sessions and play in most of the state tournaments for the year. That's a lot of weekends."

"And then ten days of play over east every year for the Nationals," Len Travers added, "and the same here for the sixth year. Most of those in the State Squad still have jobs. Getting time off work can be difficult."

"And family commitments," Romola put in. "You can't be playing in the week-end tournaments yourself if you have to cart kids around to their sporting events. And you'd never see the person you were married to unless they played as well."

There were nods all round, but Hettie sensed some of those present felt they were being challenged for not doing more.

"That's right," Judy said. "You need to be motivated and dedicated to make the commitment," Judy said. "Most of us like the challenge of competing. We like the social aspect, and its good exercise, but most of it don't want or need it to be anything more."

"You're right of course," Hettie agreed. It was a bit depressing. How could she raise the Club's profile if they remained a provincial social sports club?

"What brought this on?" Andrew asked.

"Well, I was watching the kids at school playing football during the lunch break today," Hettie told him. "And I started thinking about how someone gets to be a top player in a sport and whether anyone in our Club could do that." She wasn't about to mention her suggestion to her cousin Frank. It was probably kite-flying on her part anyway.

"Why haven't you tried out for the State Squad, Hettie?" Jo Isaacs asked. There were some nods and grins at that. As usual, Jo Isaacs had the effect of getting Hettie's hackles up.

"I will if you will," she heard herself say.

Jo grinned. "You're on, Hettie Parke. You're on."

Hettie saw looks being exchanged, as if people were wondering what was going on. She was asking herself the same question.

"I wouldn't mind giving it a try," Belle, who had been quiet up until now, spoke up. "I wouldn't mind getting some coaching and improving my game, even if I don't make it to the team. It could be fun."

"Go, Belle," Romola said.

Go, Belle, indeed, Hettie thought. "Anyone else?" she asked, looking around. She'd started this so she might as well take it as far as she could now. At least she wasn't going to be alone with Jo, now that Belle had put her hand up.

"I'll want to run it past Maree first," Tom Eastbourne said, "but I'm game."

"You're a shoo-in, Tom," Andrew told him.

"We'll see, lad. We'll see."

Hettie had been doing little more than thinking out loud when she made her comment at the start, but she could feel excitement and anticipation among her members now. She wouldn't be surprised if one or two others joined them, after doing the same as Tom had said about talking it over with their other half.

"I'll wait until Saturday," Romola said, "and then I'll send everyone's name to Richie

Bolton. He's going to be over the moon. He lives to coach players." Hettie just hoped the State Squad coach wouldn't think they were a bunch of no-hopers aiming above their skill level.

Hettie and Violet had barely walked in their front door when Elly knocked on the back door and joined them in the kitchen.

"Do you want a cocoa?" Violet asked reaching for the mugs from the shelf.

"Thanks," Elly said. She took a seat at the kitchen table and Ceefer came over to say hello. Rather distractedly, she patted his head. Hettie finished filling Ceefer's water dish and joined Elly at the table.

"So what is bothering you about Aunt Alice, love?" she asked.

"Well…this morning, the girls and I baked blueberry muffins," Elly said, "and Jaz wanted to share them with Aunt Alice, so we went to her place. But…she wouldn't let us in." Hettie frowned. "Jaz tried marching straight in as soon as the door was opened, as usual, but Aunt Alice stopped her. Practically pushed Jaz out and almost closed the door on us. She looked frightened, Mum. It scared the girls. They'd never seen her behave like that."

31

"Frightened? Really?"

Elly nodded. "I asked her what was wrong. Did she have visitors? She said she'd just shampooed the carpet and didn't want anyone walking on it while it was wet. And how about she came to our place for morning tea because she would love to try the muffins. So that's what she did, and as you saw she was still there asleep when you called in."

"Well, I suppose, if her carpet was wet. You know how house proud she is."

"You don't keep looking over your shoulder at a wet carpet, Mum," Elly said. "It's not likely to get up and attack you or run off or anything."

"Is that what she was doing? Are you sure?"

Elly nodded. "It was weird, and I didn't tell you what she did yesterday, did I?" Hettie shook her head. "Well, I'd taken the girls to the Cafe for a late breakfast, and she was standing in the front yard arguing with someone when we came back."

"Really? Who? About what?"

"There wasn't anyone there, Mum," Elly said. "She was arguing with thin air."

"Oh. She wasn't talking to one of her cats, was she? Or to her plants? I mean, I have seen her do that."

"She'd hardly say 'what do you want, why are you here', to a plant. And none of her cats were around."

"She must have been talking to someone on her phone, then." But even that didn't make sense with what Elly had overheard her saying.

"Aunt Alice doesn't have a mobile phone, Mum," Violet put in, as she placed three mugs of cocoa on the table with a marshmallow in each one.

Of course, she didn't. But she used to, didn't she? Hettie was sure she remembered a time. Had Uncle Roscoe objected to the cost? She tried to imagine Aunt Alice keeping a phone secretly but couldn't.

"Do you think she's having some sort of breakdown?" Violet asked. "She doesn't want me sleeping over anymore."

Elly frowned. "Perhaps there's someone else there already."

"That doesn't make even the slightest bit of sense, Elly."

"You wouldn't say that if you'd seen her reaction when we knocked on her door this morning," Elly said, sounding somewhat aggrieved.

"She just lost her husband five days ago, in rather tragic circumstances," Hettie reminded them. "No one acts exactly like themselves after a loss like that. She might be feeling all at odds at the moment too, because she doesn't know what to do with herself." Spring cleaning the house and shampooing the carpet to keep busy. Exhausting herself so she could sleep. "The funeral is on Friday. We'll keep an eye on her and see how she is getting on next week, okay?"

Elly agreed but wasn't altogether happy about it.

"I'm not downplaying your concerns, Elly," Hettie said, giving her a hug, "but it's early days yet. Thanks for letting us know what's been happening."

"I don't want to lose someone else," Elly said a tear in her voice. Hettie knew it wasn't Uncle Roscoe she was referring to, but her father, although Roscoe's death had likely brought it to mind. She and Brian might have been divorced but it was his fatal car accident a year ago that took him away from his daughters. And she had to admit, Aunt Alice's behaviour did seem a little bizarre, and most unlike her.

Chapter 4

The day of Uncle Roscoe's funeral dawned hot and sunny. Hettie felt herself wilting as she walked up the dry tussocky slope of the paddock to the little collection of headstones at the top. It seemed appropriate to wear a dress and heels to a funeral, but she was walking on her toes so her heels wouldn't sink into the soil and be ruined. The backs of her legs were already aching. Eddie was helping Aunt Alice who'd at least had the sense to wear flats.

"The flies are bad here," Gwen muttered, brushing at something that was buzzing around her.

"That's a bee, Auntie Gwen," Elly said, trying to redirect it with her bag. She leaned in and sniffed. "Are you wearing perfume?"

"No."

"I can smell something flowery," Elly said, giggling as the bee circled back. "So can he. It's quite strong."

"Oh, it must be the rose shower gel. Aunt Alice gave it to me for Christmas last year," she whispered. "Oh for…" She waved her hands wildly as the bee homed in again. She hit Hettie on the shoulder as she did.

"What are you doing?" she asked.

"It's a bee."

"Oh, there's another one," Violet said, joining in and flapping her hands around Gwen's head.

"Ouch, that was my ear."

"Sorry, Auntie Gwen."

"Is this a new dance craze?" Jack wanted to know, coming up behind them. He was using a four-footed cane to deal with the terrain and Larry was assisting him.

Callie scowled. "Really. It's hardly appropriate behaviour for a funeral."

"I'm sorry Callie," Gwen said, "but I'm being attacked by bees."

There were now three of the winged creatures buzzing agitatedly around Gwen. Elly tried to flick one off the top of Gwen's head.

"Don't do that," said another voice. "You'll just make them angry."

"Hello, Mrs. Bronson," Violet greeted the elderly woman.

"Hello Vi, dear. Edith," Mrs. Bronson said, turning to her companion, "do you have that lime spray with you?"

"Somewhere in here," said Mrs. Braxton, already scrabbling in her large bag. "I know I have it here somewhere. Ah..." She held up an old-fashioned glass perfume atomiser. "Close your eyes," she said to Gwen.

With several puffs from the atomiser, a light lime-smelling mist settled over Gwen's hair and clothes. Gwen sneezed as three puzzled bees beat a hasty retreat.

"Wow. That's amazing," Gwen said, opening her eyes to find nothing buzzing around her. "Thank you."

"No trouble, dear. My Albert was allergic to bee stings among other things, feathers and what not, so I always carried some anti-dots. Never bothered to throw them out after."

Jack cleared his throat, trying not to smile, Hettie thought, at Mrs. Braxton's mangling of the word antidote.

"Crisis over," he said. "We'd best be moving on. I can see our Reverend looking rather impatient up there."

"At least he's in the shade," Callie grumbled.

Mrs. Braxton immediately attached herself to Frank while Mrs. Bronson took Rafe's arm to help her up the hill. Elly winked at him from his other side and he grinned before putting his nose in the air. Hettie and Gwen supported one another, and they made it over the tussocks to the top of the hill and the scant shade from the scrubby mallee eucalypts with their thick twisted trunks. They looked to have been there forever.

Jack greeted the Reverend, shaking hands and apologising for the delay. Their behaviour on the way up must have looked odd. A little behind the minister a group of four men from the undertakers stood, hands clasped before them, in respectful pose. In another setting Hettie imagined them as somebody's minders or bodyguards. In a way, they were already.

The Reverend looked around the gathered group and waited as a latecomer hurried the last little distance. It was Aunt Alice's neighbour, Lil Walters. Nice of her to bother, Hettie thought.

Aunt Alice waited stoically by the edge of the grave, where the coffin lay ready to be lowered. Hettie wondered how difficult it must have been to get it up the slope. Jack stood on Aunt Alice's left with Callie beside him. Hettie was about to fill the space on her aunt's right, when Mrs. Bronson took a tentative step forward, before glancing sideways at Hettie.

Hettie nodded and smiled and gave a little forward movement with her hand. Aunt Alice would feel better with a friend her own age beside her. She certainly wasn't going to get any comfort from her sister-in-law.

The Reverend spoke his piece, the solemn, time-old words washing over those present. He added a few words about Roscoe and Aunt Alice, then the coffin was lowered by the undertakers' men and Aunt Alice tossed the first handful of soil from the pile beside the grave. It landed with a soft thud. Others gradually did the same before standing around awkwardly as the Reverend spoke to Aunt Alice privately.

As Hettie turned away from the grave, she saw Sergeant Stuart Higgins standing at the back of the group.

"I didn't expect to see you here," Hettie said joining him.

"I've never been to a graveside service before," Stuart said. "I guess this was how it was always done years ago."

"I guess so," Hettie agreed scanning the little cemetery.

The graves of her grandparents were obvious by the newness of the memorial stones, and there was a low decorative metal border surrounding their joint plot. There were several older weathered stones, one or two leaning a little.

"This land was part of the original land grant," Hettie told him. "The oldest burial goes back to the eighteen-sixties. My grandfather had this paddock fenced off so the graves weren't disturbed."

"Uh huh. Do they know of everyone who's buried here? There are obviously more graves here than those marked with the gravestones."

"I doubt if anyone knows who all of them belong to now," Hettie said. "Many would have had just a wooden cross, but they'd have rotted away years ago." She could see several smaller bumps that must have belonged to child burials but not all those would be obvious now either. She pointed out one or two of the more obvious ones to Stuart.

"There were a lot of infant deaths back before the healthy living conditions and modern medicine we enjoy now. I remember reading about an outbreak of typhoid back in the eighteen-nineties when all the children in one family were ill. The parents came back from burying one child to find another had died in their absence. It must have been heartbreaking." Stuart murmured agreement.

"Hettie?" Larry called, gesturing that they were leaving. She lifted her hand in acknowledgement.

"There's food on offer at the Sunny Vale Community Centre," she told Stuart as they started back down to the road, where they had left their cars. "You're welcome to join us."

"Thanks, but I was stretching my time just to come here. It's been interesting though."

As she drove the two miles back into Woody Lake, Hettie couldn't shake the nagging feeling that seeing a graveside funeral in an old cemetery wasn't the main reason Stuart Higgins had been there.

There was a large gathering of people in the reception rooms of the Sunny Vale Community Centre when Hettie arrived. She'd dropped Violet off and then driven across the Road to leave her car in her own driveway before walking back. Parking at Sunny Vale was at a premium today and cars already lined one side of the Road near the entrance to the place.

The double doors of both the living room and dining room were open on either side of the entrance hall. The rooms looked beautiful, with huge arrangements of greenery, red flowering bottlebrush, and yellow banksia and grevillea, dotted with purple hovea.

Food was arranged on the table in the

dining room, while Aunt Alice sat at the far end of the living room on a long sofa with several armchairs arranged nearby. Jack and Eddie sat on either side of Aunt Alice with Callie in an armchair closer to Jack. Conversation in the room was muted as people moved back and forth, collecting food and drink, forming groups then breaking apart to form others. Hettie doubted if many of them had even known Roscoe Slater, but they all knew the Parke family in some form or other.

She looked around for Larry and saw him talking to Joel Chauncy, his accountant for the Parke Real Estate Agency. She crossed the room to join them.

"Hello Joel," Hettie said. "Would you excuse us a moment. I need to speak to Larry."

Joel nodded somewhat stiffly. They didn't have the best of relationships since she'd revealed his connection to a murderer not long ago. Larry waited for her to speak as Joel moved away.

"Do you know if Pop has heard anything final about Uncle Roscoe's death?" Hettie asked him.

"We've not heard the result of the autopsy, if that's what you mean. You're not looking for a problem, I hope."

"You did notice Sergeant Higgins at the

funeral, didn't you?"

"Mmm. I did wonder if you'd added another police officer to your personal entourage."

Hettie shook her head. "No, and I can assure you he wasn't there because of me. Could you chat to that group of men." She indicated a group of five, looking slightly uncomfortable, glasses of some amber liquid in their hands. One man was carrying a brown paper shopping bag. "Men's Shed, I think. See if you can find out what they were all doing Saturday morning."

"What aren't you telling me, Sis?"

"I'm a little uneasy, is all. This is the perfect opportunity to talk to those fellows so I think we should take advantage of it."

"As far as I know," Larry said lowering his voice. "No one could have got into Aunt Alice's backyard on Saturday unless they went through the house."

"I don't think that's been established for certain. Uncle Roscoe could have let someone in that Aunt Alice didn't know about."

Someone who could have left through her backyard. Neither she nor Violet were at home, and a person could access the Road from down either side of her house. Larry raised his eyebrows but went to speak to the Men's Shed group. She might be overthinking it, but it was always better to be prepared. Like right now, as Dan Wallace, reporter for the *Rosny Record,* appeared at her side.

He was a presentable young man in his late twenties, tallish and slim with a cheeky smile. It probably stood him in good stead in his line of work. He'd been a great help in solving an earlier death she'd been involved in.

"I've just spoken to Mrs. Slater," he said. "I'll do a small piece on the funeral, but I didn't want to bother her for information. Thought you'd be a better source. I might send my photographer out to the cemetery for some atmosphere, if that's okay."

"Ah, would you mind not doing that, Dan, please? The cemetery is isolated, so its location is best not made widely known. Less chance of anyone doing damage to what's left there." She was aware of the fencing and locked gates around Perth's pioneer cemetery, and that was in a populated central suburb.

Dan nodded. "I suppose so. I can write about it, though, can't I?"

Hettie said of course he could, just not reveal details of the location. He thanked her and walked off. She went to join her parents and Aunt Alice, making her way across the room, pausing several times to exchange a few words.

"You mustn't let Violet get too friendly with that man," her mother said as Hettie took the empty seat beside her. Callie nodded in the direction of the patio. In full view through the French doors, Hettie saw Violet in animated conversation with Dan Wallace.

"Oh, Dan's alright," Hettie found herself saying. Or perhaps she was just disagreeing with her mother, she wasn't sure.

"We don't need his sort," Callie said.

"They're just having a conversation, Mum."

"It has to start somewhere."

"Mmm. But you must admit, Dan did a decent article about Craig Lewis' death. Especially as it turned out to be a domestic issue and nothing to do with the Clubs."

Dan had added a paragraph about her proposed expansion of the croquet courts at the Parke Club, and how it would bring a national sporting event to Woody Lake. They had garnered a good number of participants in their last 'Introduction to Croquet Course' as a result.

"Our name still came up in connection," Callie carped. "Perhaps it's time the name was changed, and we had nothing to do with the place at all."

Hettie felt the creases on her forehead growing deeper, as she struggled to keep her promise to herself not to bite back when her mother made such comments. Besides, this wasn't the time or place for an argument. Fortunately a distraction arrived in the form of Larry with the Men's Shed members, before she could be tested further.

One of the men, a grey-haired, stocky man in his sixties, was carrying a small wooden box. He introduced himself to Aunt Alice as Jim something-or-other. Hettie didn't catch the full name.

"Roscoe was making this for you," Jim told her. "We finished it for you, and my wife did the lining inside."

"How very kind of you," Aunt Alice replied taking the item. It was a small jewellery box made of jarrah, the rich red tones of the wood contrasting with the diamond-shaped insert in the lid, which was in a lighter, honey-coloured timber. Aunt Alice opened the box to reveal the deep-blue velvet lining. "It's beautiful. Roscoe loved small timber pieces. Treen, he called them. Please thank your wife for her trouble, too."

"I will," Jim replied. "She said to tell you she would like to call on you at some time."

"Oh. Of course. I'm, I'm not taking callers

for a while, please tell her."

Jim nodded. The other Men's Shed members spoke a few words to Aunt Alice and then, relieved at having done their duty, they wandered away.

Hettie stood and joined Larry. "Nothing doing there, Sis," he said. "Seems they were visiting the Men's Shed at Burns Beach on Saturday morning. Roscoe had decided not to go. It wasn't said outright, but I got the impression he hadn't wanted to pay a share of the minibus hire."

"Well, that takes them off the list of possible suspects then. As far as I know, Uncle Roscoe didn't have any other social outlet here except for our family."

Hettie noticed the Men's Shed members had moved to the dining room where the food was laid out. Aside from offering criticism, her mother excelled at arranging beautiful and fitting events.

Chapter 5

The weekend went by quietly. Aunt Alice seemed calmer and more settled with Roscoe buried and the formalities dealt with. But she still looked tired and drawn. She came to dinner with Hettie and Violet Sunday night but went home early. Hettie didn't see her in the garden when she left for work next day. She hoped her aunt was still asleep.

"That seemed to go off well on Friday," Frank commented at morning recess as they helped themselves to coffee and a biscuit in the staff room. "How is Aunt Alice doing now?"

"Still tired, but she came to dinner last night," Hettie said, choosing an armchair off to the side away from the main table. She hadn't spoken to Frank, or to anyone else in the family yet about Elly's concerns. They were playing a watching brief. It had only been ten days since Roscoe's accident after all.

"Mmmh. Dad told me yesterday that he saw her in the park on Thursday night, around eleven," Frank said taking the armchair next to her and putting his plate containing several biscuits on the small table in front of them.

"That late?" Hettie said. "She's usually in bed by then. Did he speak to her?"

Frank nodded. "He saw her safely back home. She wouldn't let him inside though, which he found a bit odd." Hettie was saddened to hear it. It seemed to be further confirmation of how Elly had said she was behaving. It was worrying to say the least.

"Did she say what she was doing in the park at that hour?"

"Something about needing to clear her head. She was sitting on the bench beside the lake, nearest the Road, so not far away from the house."

"That's something I suppose. At least she wasn't just wandering around. But what was Eddie doing out there at that time of night?"

"One guess," Frank said, with a half-laugh. "He was keeping an eye on dear Aunt Gloria. She's convinced the government has night-vision cameras set up everywhere to spy on us. She was searching for them in the park with some new gizmo she bought on the internet."

"Oh my. I suppose that's a change from the drones the government is supposed to be using anyway. Poor Eddie. Does she need her medication increased?"

Frank shook his head. "He tried that before, but she was little better than a zombie. He'd rather deal with her occasional delusions."

Hettie could understand that, but it must be tiring and more than a little stressful at times. She wondered if Aunt Alice needed some medication to get her through Roscoe's death. Getting her to admit as much and to see a doctor, though, would be another matter.

Aunt Alice was sitting out front of her house on her garden bench when Hettie pulled into her driveway after work. As Hettie got out of her car, Aunt Alice came across to her.

"How are you doing?" Hettie asked, pulling her into a hug.

"I'm fine, thank you dear." Hettie didn't believe her for a moment. She wasn't looking any more well-rested than she had Sunday evening, and her face was almost haggard. Was she losing weight as well? "I'm glad you're home," Aunt Alice said. "That Sergeant Higgins is coming to interview me soon and I didn't want to see him on my own."

"Is he? I'll come over to your house, then."

"Oh, no. The house is in a mess right now. I've started sorting out Roscoe's things. Can we see him at yours?"

Hettie frowned. The evidence was growing for Elly's claim that Aunt Alice wasn't allowing anyone in her house.

"Ah, yes, sure," she replied. "We'll put a note on your door letting Stuart know where you are then, shall we?" Aunt Alice nodded.

After dealing with the note, Hettie made tea for her aunt and coffee for herself, and they sat down at the kitchen table to wait. There was half a chocolate cake in the fridge, courtesy of Violet and Hettie put some slices on a plate. They didn't have long to wait, but Stuart didn't seem pleased to be interviewing Aunt Alice at Hettie's place with her present. Hettie wasn't about to excuse herself, but she had the distinct feeling she was on notice.

"Now, Mrs. Slater," Stuart said when he was seated with coffee and a slice of cake, as well as his notebook, "I need to clarify a few points before we can finalise this matter. Very briefly, you told me you were vacuuming the floors while your husband was out cleaning the gutters. You came into the dining room and saw the gutter hanging outside the kitchen window. You then went out to see what had happened, and found the ladder on the ground, and your husband lying over the wheelbarrow. He didn't appear to be breathing, and you called an ambulance. Correct?"

"Yes, that's what happened."

"Alright. Can you tell me what time your husband went out to clean the gutters?"

"It was after breakfast, around nine I suppose."

"And do you know what time it was when you went outside and found him?"

Aunt Alice shook her head. "I've no idea."

"But you called the ambulance immediately?" Aunt Alice stared down at the table. Stuart waited but she didn't answer.

"Did you go for help?" Hettie prompted. "Lil said…"

"If you try putting words in her mouth, I will take Mrs. Slater to the station to continue this interview," Stuart said sharply. Hettie flinched but kept quiet.

Aunt Alice roused herself. "Well, I guess so."

"What do you mean, you guess so?"

"I went out front," Aunt Alice told him. "I went up to your door Hettie, but then I remembered you'd still be at the Club. I didn't want to call Elly, but then I thought Rafe might be home, so I was just going to go there when I saw Lil coming back from walking Howie. She said I looked lost and asked what was wrong. When I told her what had happened, she went to check for herself, and when she came back, she rang for the ambulance."

"So, Ms. Walters went into your backyard? Was she gone long, Mrs. Slater?"

"Oh, a few minutes, I suppose."

"And what happened after she called the ambulance?"

"Well, we waited for it to arrive," Aunt Alice said, as if that should be obvious.

"Did you go to the backyard with the ambulance officers?"

"No. Lil showed them the way. And then Elly came when she heard the ambulance, and then Hettie and Violet, and then you did."

Stuart nodded and made some more notes. He took a sip of his coffee.

"Does that explain everything?" Hettie ventured hopefully.

"How did Mrs. Walters get to the backyard?" Stuart asked, answering Hettie's question by asking another.

"She went through the house. The front gate was locked. I told you that before."

"And did she take the dog with her?" Stuart went on.

Aunt Alice frowned. "Yes, she did. I thought it odd, but she probably didn't even realise she was still holding his leash, and he just went along."

"And the ambulance officers. Did they go through the house too?"

"Yes." Stuart made another note.

"What did the ambulance officers have to say about the gate?" Hettie asked. "They must know if it was locked or not, as they came out that way."

"The gate was locked," Stuart said briskly. "The only access to the backyard was through the house." Hettie didn't think she liked the sound of that.

"Now, Mrs. Slater," he went on, "here's my problem. According to a witness and confirmed by the autopsy, it's understood that your husband fell off the ladder sometime around nine thirty. The ambulance wasn't called until ten minutes to twelve. What were you doing during those two-and-a-half hours?" Aunt Alice remained silent.

"Mrs. Slater," Stuart said, his voice rising, "are you telling me, that you were vacuuming the house for almost three hours before you came into the dining room and saw the gutter hanging down?"

"No...I don't think so."

"What time was it when you found him?"

"I don't know."

"When did you put the vacuum cleaner away, Mrs. Slater?"

The vacuum cleaner. That's what Hettie had missed when they were leaving Aunt Alice's house that morning. Her aunt must have tidied up after finding her husband dead. Unless – she hadn't been vacuuming at all.

Aunt Alice stared down at her cup, her fingers curling around it. "I thought I must have been dreaming and I'd wake up soon," she said, her voice barely above a whisper. "Roscoe would finish cleaning the gutters and he'd come in for a cup of tea, all pleased with himself. I seem to remember finishing the floors, putting the vacuum cleaner away. I may have mopped the kitchen floor. I'm not sure. I just pottered about for a while. I know I made tea, but that," she gulped, "that gutter was still hanging there outside the window."

She took a breath, and her words came faster. "Eventually I had to go out and see if Roscoe wanted a cuppa, and all the while I was afraid that what I'd dreamt was real. And it was. And see, I'd warned him. It was like I'd wished it." She looked up, glancing at Stuart and Hettie as if begging them to understand. "I felt responsible."

There was silence. Hettie reached out and squeezed Aunt Alice's hand, to heck with Stuart. Even he should be able to see she was telling the truth.

"What did you do then?" Stuart asked.

"I went out front to tell someone, like I said. That's when Lil found me."

Stuart made some more notes. "Is that all you've got to say?"

"It's what happened."

"Who was the witness?" Hettie asked. "Was someone in the backyard after all?"

"The neighbour at the back heard a shout and a crash around nine thirty," Stuart replied. "According to him, a man's voice shouted what sounded like 'Alice,' and then there was silence. He called out but got no answer, and decided it wasn't any of his business."

"Henry Dunlop," Aunt Alice said. "Roscoe couldn't abide him. He cut off branches from our trees and shrubs that hung over the fence and tossed them back into our yard."

"How did the autopsy pinpoint the time of death?" Hettie asked.

"Time of death was calculated by the digestion of food in the stomach," Stuart said, "based on the time Mrs. Slater said her husband had gone out, and by the lividity, which is the way blood pools in the lower part of the body when circulation stops. It becomes clearer after a few days. What the autopsy discovered on both counts concurs with the witness report. Do you have anything to add now, Mrs. Slater?" Aunt Alice shook her head. Stuart closed his notebook. "Thank you. I shouldn't need to trouble you again."

Alice gave a dispirited nod back. Stuart got to his feet and Hettie followed him into the hall.

"So, Uncle Roscoe's death is officially an accident?" she said as he stepped out onto the porch.

Stuart didn't look at her. "Death by misadventure. Sometimes there just isn't the evidence for any other verdict. G'day, Hettie." He walked off to his police car parked on the street.

Hettie quietly closed the door. She didn't need it spelt out. Sergeant Stuart Higgins had his own suspicions about Roscoe Slater's death, and they didn't include an accident. She'd been right to be suspicious about his presence at the funeral. She went back to the kitchen.

"I know he doesn't believe me, Hettie," Aunt Alice said sadly. "He thinks I had something to do with it."

"No, I'm sure that's not true," Hettie rushed to assure her. "He just needed to get the details for his report, like he said. He told me it's being declared death by misadventure."

Aunt Alice looked at her, clear-eyed if a

little shaky. "What if I did do it and I've blocked it from my mind?" She looked away. "He must be here for some reason," she muttered.

"He was, but it's finished now. It's taken care of. You are staying for dinner I hope?"

"What? Oh, no. I think I might go home, dear. Don't worry about dinner. I'm, I just need to rest."

"Did you get something from your doctor to help you sleep, like I suggested?"

"I've got some lavender oil."

"Alright, but if you change your mind about dinner, just come over. You know you're always welcome. You don't need to wait for an invitation."

"I do, dear. Thank you. But I'm fine, really."

Hettie didn't believe her for one single moment. It was time for a family meeting.

Chapter 6

"So, Stuart Higgins suspects Aunt Alice of having something to do with Roscoe falling off his ladder," Larry said, when Hettie finished telling them about yesterday's interview with the Sergeant, as well as explaining about Aunt Alice's recent behaviour.

They were sitting over the remains of a Chinese takeaway at Hettie's house. Ceefer had already inhaled the pieces of lemon chicken Hettie had put in his bowl and was hanging about for any more handouts or pieces 'accidentally' dropped on the floor.

"I know she's been behaving out of sorts, for her," Rafe said. His chair was pushed back from the table, Rosa asleep against his shoulder. "Perhaps all this time she's been frightened the police will find out about those missing hours and suspect her of being responsible. And now they have, and they do. I should think that fear would make anyone behave oddly."

There were several nods to this, but Elly

didn't agree. "Odd doesn't cover not letting us in her house. There's someone else involved."

"You mean, someone who perhaps knows what Aunt Alice did?" Gwen said, sounding doubtful. "Or someone who caused it, and Aunt Alice knows?"

"I know it sounds awful, whichever way," Elly replied, "but... that's what it feels like, Auntie Gwen. Given everything."

"So, she could be protecting someone."

"She'd protect one of us," Hettie said, "but she wouldn't be frightened of us. Besides, only you and Rafe were around that morning."

"We were. Maxxie called in for half an hour. It was that Saturday, wasn't it?" Elly asked Rafe.

"Yes, but he'd left before we heard the ambulance."

"Did you have a tradie in for any work that morning?" Hettie asked, feeling she was grasping at straws. Rafe shook his head.

"The police can't have any real doubts if they've officially passed it as an accident," Larry declared.

"Stuart does have doubts, Larry," Hettie said. "That's the point. But it's more a case of his not having any hard evidence to prove it being anything other than an accident."

"I'm sure that happens more often than

people think," Gwen said. "Murders that get passed off as accidents or suicide for lack of evidence. I've heard of the police believing they know who did something but unable to prove it."

"And also believing someone did something when they didn't," Hettie said. "Innocent people get convicted too. It's not a perfect system. It's run by humans, after all." There was a moment's silence as everyone digested what that could mean. "But it's more than that. It's Aunt Alice. She's going to completely fall apart if she goes on like this. She could end up in hospital, or in the Nursing Home because she's unable to take care of herself."

"It does seem more than just grief," Gwen said.

"Mrew?"

"Even Ceefer's concerned," she added, reaching down to rub his head.

Larry gave a 'tsk.' He wasn't ready to accept that Ceefer understood what was being said.

"So, what do we have?' he asked. "More than two hours between Aunt Alice finding Roscoe dead and calling an ambulance." He ticked it off on his fingers. "Not letting anyone in her house for the past week. Appearing nervous, sometimes frightened. Sleeping poorly. Is that it?" Everyone agreed it was. "Well, before we make too much of all this, we need to ask Aunt Alice to explain."

"You make it sound perfectly simple," Hettie said.

"It is."

"Only if she will talk to us, and she hasn't been very forthcoming to date. Quite the opposite, in fact."

Larry put down his coffee mug and got to his feet. "Well, there's no time like the present."

"As much as we would like to go with you, we need to get the girls to bed," Rafe said, getting to his feet. "Let us know how it goes." Elly was clearly torn between needing to put Rosa to bed and being involved.

"I'll call in on our way home and let you know how it goes," Gwen promised her niece. Elly thanked her and she and Rafe left.

Aunt Alice's front porch light was on, and all was quiet, when Hettie, Larry and Gwen reached her door. Not even the sound of the television penetrated to the outside. Hettie rang the doorbell. After a moment, with no response, Gwen slipped along to the living room window where a strip of light leaked out between the curtains.

"Can't see anyone," she whispered. "And

the television's not on."

Hettie rang the bell again. "Perhaps she's gone out." She looked around into the semi-darkness of the park. As she did, three figures appeared, walking toward them.

"Mum?" Violet queried. Dan was with her. And Aunt Alice.

"There you are," Gwen said to Aunt Alice. "We were worried about you."

"Me? Honestly, there's no need," she replied. "I'm fine."

Hettie and Larry exchanged a look. "We wanted to make sure," Larry told her. "Can we come in for a chat?"

"Oh, no. The place is a mess."

"Your house is never a mess," Hettie said.

"It is. I've been clearing out Roscoe's things. He had so much stuff."

"But we're family," Larry said. "The mess isn't important to us. You are. We understand what you're going through."

"And you don't have to be doing that all by yourself," Hettie said. "We can help. I'm sure it must be difficult."

"I just do a little bit each day," Aunt Alice assured them. She unlocked her front door and stood with her hand on the doorknob. "It's, um, cathartic. You know, letting go, clearing my head space as the young people say."

"Is that why you were in the park?" Gwen asked.

"I just needed to get out for a bit."

"I'm not sure I like the idea of you wandering around out here by yourself at this time of night," Larry added.

"Oh, pish. No one is interested in an old woman. I just needed some fresh air. I appreciate your concern, really, it's very sweet of you, but you need to stop fussing. I'm fine," she said, "and right now I'm going to bed. Goodnight." She stepped inside quickly shutting the door behind her. The snip of the deadlock as it was engaged reached them clearly.

"That went well, I don't think," Hettie said, as they all stared at the closed door.

"Short of forcing our way in, there wasn't much we could do," Gwen said.

"No, and we could make matters worse, if we were to do that," Larry said thoughtfully.

Hettie was suddenly aware of Dan, watching and listening with interest.

"How are you, Dan?" she said now.

"I'm fine, thanks," he replied. Everyone was silent. "Ah, well." He turned to Violet. "I might pop into the Cafe for lunch tomorrow," he said. "I'll, uh, see you then."

"Sure," Violet replied and sent her mother

a look as Dan walked off to where his car was parked nearby on the street.

"Sorry Vi, but this is family business," Hettie told her, as they crossed back to her front yard.

"Where did you find her, Vi?" Larry asked.

"She was sitting on the first bench by the lake. What were you all doing?"

Larry held the door, and they trooped back inside.

"We were hoping to talk to her about what's been bothering her lately," Hettie said.

"She wasn't exactly pleased when we found her in the park and I said we'd walk her back home. But I think she'd been crying, Mum."

"Well, that's not surprising, love. She has just lost her husband."

And now Aunt Alice was alone in her house with her memories. Unless she did have someone else in there. Someone she didn't want anyone else to know about. Their meal leftovers were still on the table and Hettie busied herself clearing them off, while everyone else congregated in the living room.

"So, what are we going to do," Gwen asked. "I mean, if we can't bust in and catch whoever it is, if it is someone."

"We'll have to keep an eye on her," Larry said. "Make sure she doesn't go walking in the park late at night by herself, anyway. I know it's pretty safe around here, but it doesn't pay to take risks either, especially at her age."

Hettie sat down on the sofa and Ceefer leapt up beside her. She absently stroked his back as he curled himself into a ball.

"But this isn't normal grieving," Hettie said. "Is it? I mean…"

Violet gasped. "You don't think Aunt Alice pushed the ladder, do you?"

"No, of course not," Hettie said, though she wasn't sure, not really. "But we're afraid she might know something, or someone else knows something, and she's… frightened."

"Oh. My. Gosh. That's even worse. I'm going to see her." Violet jumped to her feet. "I'll stay with her again tonight. She was fine with that last week." Violet hurried off to her room and reappeared a few minutes later with her overnight bag. "See you in the morning," she said, and they heard the back door open and close.

"If she lets Vi in, we'll know she doesn't have anyone else in there," Hettie said.

"At the moment, anyway," Larry said. They chatted in a desultory fashion as they waited. As the minutes passed, they began to relax.

Larry yawned. "Time for bed I'm

thinking."

The sound of the back door opening and closing brought them back to the moment. Violet came into the living room, eyes wide, worry lines creasing her forehead.

"Oh, Vi." Hettie got to her feet and pulled her into a hug.

"Who's in there?" she wanted to know, tears in her voice. "What is she afraid of?"

"You think she really is afraid of something?" Hettie asked.

"She kept looking over her shoulder. Mum, I talked, I begged her to let me in. She said she couldn't. It would only cause trouble."

"That's it," Larry said. "This calls for action. We need an intervention. We need to get her to talk to us."

"Isn't that what we just tried?" Hettie said.

"We were hardly well prepared, Sis. And that reporter was there. Why don't you invite her over for dinner tomorrow night, and we'll all be here? In the meantime, we'll plan what we need to say to her."

"It isn't going to be easy," Gwen warned. "She knows we've noticed. She's going to be on the defensive now."

"Gwen's right," Hettie said. "I think we need to stop fussing about her first. It isn't working anyway. What if we let her think we accept what she's told us about being okay? Give her time to realise she actually does need our help. Just for a few days," she added. "We'll keep an eye on her, just not let her know we are."

"I'm not sure waiting is a good idea if someone else is involved," Larry said.

"Do you want to break in? You said yourself that might make matters worse. And Aunt Alice just told Violet the same thing. It's too risky."

"Hettie's right, Larry," Gwen told him. "We need to be patient. And strategic."

Larry rubbed his hand over his head in frustration. Like most men, if there was something wrong he wanted to fix it. "Alright. I'll check the park each night and keep a watch if she's there."

"What about dinner Friday, then? Three days?" Hettie asked. "Do you think that's long enough?"

"We can only try," Gwen said. It was agreed.

"I might invite her to go for a walk before dinner Friday," Hettie said. "Walking in the dark often loosens a person's tongue."

"Is that what it does," Larry said, and smirked, but his attempt to be funny fell flat.

Chapter 7

That evening, the Channel Seven news had an item on a shoplifting spree that seemed to be gathering momentum through the northern Perth suburbs. The police admitted they were struggling and appealed for help from the public, especially from parents, as it appeared someone was recruiting children for the shoplifting. There'd been an article on it in the previous issue of the *Rosny Record*, too, so Hettie wasn't surprised when Stuart Higgins turned up at Rosny Primary School next day.

He spoke to several of the older classes including Hettie's Grade Five. He talked about shoplifting in general, and that while it might seem like a fun lark, it was stealing, pure and simple, and could lead to other crimes and time in prison. If his intent was to frighten, Hettie thought he had succeeded from the expressions on the faces of her eleven-year-old students.

"What do you think is happening?" Ann Potter, the deputy headmistress, asked as she put a cup of coffee and a ham sandwich in front of Stuart when he joined them in the staff room at lunch time.

"It seems to be an organised band," he told them. "We've picked up a couple of kids who were caught in the act, but they don't know anything about who is recruiting them or aren't saying. We haven't got anything that can lead us to them yet." He swallowed a mouthful of sandwich and washed it down with some coffee. "Joondalup nabbed a ten-year-old who'd lifted some pricey perfume at Myers," he went on. "A present for his mum he said. Which could be true, of course, but it also fits with other items that have been stolen – small, expensive, easy to pocket. Needless to say, we need to stop it. It means kids getting lured into a life of crime, a black market that attracts more serious players. Even turf wars."

"Not to mention higher insurance rates for retailers resulting in higher prices," Ann added.

Stuart nodded. "I've no doubt there's at least one group in your fifth and sixth grade classes involved. Three or four students, boys and girls, sometimes working together."

Hettie's mind skipped through the faces she saw each day. Was it Paul, who rarely opened his mouth, Polly who never shut up, or Ava the clever one? They could be loyal and secretive at that age, their morals still in the formative stage, with adults perceived as almost another species. But it angered her to think someone was exploiting these kids.

"Some sort of Fagan operation," she commented.

"Fagan?"

"A Charles Dickens character. Fagan had a street gang of young pick pockets."

"I know who Fagan is, Hettie. Cops do read you know."

"Of course, they do," Hettie replied. She felt on quicksand at the moment where Stuart was concerned. Better not dig a deeper hole for herself. These things weren't forgotten in the staff room, either.

"We're urging parents to keep an eye out for unexplained spending," Stuart added.

"I don't believe it," Third Grade teacher Marcia Gibbons said. "This has been going on for weeks already. No kid is going to hide money away for weeks and not spend it."

"Huh. You'd only need one to show off the latest toy they'd bought and the whole thing would fall down like a house of cards," Ann Potter agreed.

"I don't know," Frank said. "The little blighters can be very canny when they want to."

"Some certainly," Ann agreed. "But as I said, it would just take one to say something."

"But would the parents report any suspicions they might have to the police?" someone else asked.

"No way. They'd protect the kid," Frank said. There were murmurs of agreement at that.

"Hence our problem," Stuart said. He finished his coffee and nodded to the room. "I would appreciate if you kept your eyes peeled and your ears to the ground," he said.

Hettie was glad no one was tempted to say, 'and try working in that position.'

Lil was coming down the street with Howie on his leash when Hettie arrived home. The woman waved and kept on past her own house toward her.

"How are you?" Hettie asked as Lil came up her driveway. Howie sniffed and raised his leg on her letterbox. Perhaps he could smell cat.

"I'm well, thanks, Hettie. Is Alice alright?" she asked, concern tinging her voice.

"As well as can be expected, I guess," Hettie replied.

"Huh. I called in this morning, but she said she'd just shampooed the carpet, and would I mind terribly if she didn't ask me in. I was sure she'd told me last week she'd cleaned the carpet. Anyway, I invited her to my place for morning tea instead. She seems a little jumpy. Have you noticed?"

"She's not herself, Lil," Hettie said. "We're keeping an eye on her. She did say she was clearing stuff out, too, so she's probably embarrassed about anyone seeing the place in a bit of a mess."

"Friends don't care about things like that," Lil replied.

"You're right about that, but Aunt Alice does. I'm sure she appreciates your friendship."

Lil sighed. "I feel really bad for her losing Roscoe like that. I took her a casserole on Monday. I know she's having dinner with you sometimes, but I thought it would be easy for her to heat up for lunch."

Hettie wished she'd thought to do the same, except right now they weren't doing anything for her. And it would be Violet doing the cooking in any case.

"That's very thoughtful of you. I'm sure Aunt Alice appreciates it. Are you working right now?" Hettie asked now. Lil always seemed to be around, and she knew nothing about her.

"Oh, I'm in between jobs right now," Li said vaguely. "Listen, I thought I might see if Alice wants to come out for the day tomorrow. Do you think she would? I need to go to Joondalup to see someone about work but that won't take more than half an hour."

"You can only ask," Hettie said.

"I believe she's going on that river cruise with Eddie and his friends. That's this Thursday isn't it?"

Hettie had forgotten all about that. So much for their plan to leave Aunt Alice to her own devices. She wasn't even going to miss them.

So it proved, when she invited Aunt Alice over for dinner on Friday. Her aunt told her she would be at Ila Bronson's house that evening, with Lil, and Edith Braxton. She eventually agreed to join the family for dinner at Hettie's house at six-thirty on Sunday.

So, on Sunday, half an hour before Aunt Alice was due to come over, Hettie presented herself at her aunt's front door.

"A walk?" Aunt Alice said, when Hettie explained why she was there.

"It's lovely and fresh out," Hettie said. "The heat has lifted, and Ceefer wants a walk before dinner."

"It is nice," Aunt Alice said, stepping out.

She pulled her keys from her pocket and turned to lock the door. Hettie noted she had never bothered to do that on previous evening walks, but then Uncle Roscoe had always been at home before.

"And how are you, Ceefer?" Aunt Alice asked tucking her hand inside Hettie's arm as they crossed the Road to the park.

"Meroow."

"I'm glad to hear it."

Hettie let Ceefer's leash out a little so he could explore along the edge of the lake where the solar powered lights lit up patches of reeds and water grasses. The evening air was punctuated by the occasional watery plop, and in the distance the faint sound of a train reached them, disappearing toward the city.

"So how have you been this week?" Hettie asked. "I've barely seen you. You've become quite the gadabout."

"I feel as if I have, too, Hettie. It's been lovely. And Lil gets on so well with Ila and Edith, too."

"Well, that's nice. Where did you go on Wednesday? Lil said she was taking you out for the day."

"We went window shopping in Joondalup and had a lovely afternoon tea with cream cakes and jam tarts. Lil was seeing someone about a job. Did I tell you Morris called me? Said he'd heard about Roscoe and would I like him to visit."

"And do you?"

"I might go visit him soon," Aunt Alice said. "I wonder what Maureen has done with my old garden?"

"I'm sure she's looking after it almost as well as you did," Hettie said. Aunt Alice smiled.

They walked on, until they reached the Clubhouse, the under-eave lights giving the building a welcoming glow.

Aunt Alice chatted about how they'd all enjoyed the river cruise, and what she would be doing in the next few days. Hettie began to think they might have it all wrong. Perhaps Aunt Alice had just needed time to come to terms with Roscoe's death. She seemed cheerful enough tonight. As they got closer to home, they heard a dog barking.

"That'll be Howie," Aunt Alice said. "Snuggly is probably sitting on the fence teasing him."

"I don't hear Howie very much. Not as much as when Lil first moved in anyway."

"No, I don't either. Lil locks him inside when she goes out now. He digs up the garden when he's left on his own, she says. Oh, I almost forgot. I baked an apple strudel today, too. I was going to bring it over for dessert, and if there's anything left, I'll take it to Lil's for afternoon tea tomorrow."

Hettie laughed. "You expect there to be some left with Larry around?" She was wondering how she could discreetly let the others know they should hold off on the intervention, when Aunt Alice suddenly stopped at the edge of her garden.

"Um, you go on home, Hettie," she said. "I don't think I'll come for dinner after all. I'm suddenly feeling rather tired."

"What, no strudel?" Hettie asked, pretending to be dismayed at missing out. She certainly hadn't missed the way her aunt's hand had tightened on her arm.

"I really am tired, I'm sorry," Aunt Alice said casting a quick glance toward her house.

"I don't believe you," Hettie said, feeling as if she'd been duped by her aunt's bright manner. "Aunt Alice, it's perfectly clear something isn't right with you. What is going on?"

"There's nothing wrong, Hettie, I told you. And you've no right to speak to me that way."

Hettie took in a deep breath and tried to keep her voice calm. "Your family are not the only ones who are concerned about your behaviour you know. Lil has been concerned about you too."

Aunt Alice bristled. "Are people talking about me?"

"Your family and friends are worried about you, Auntie. They can see something is wrong. What is it?"

"It's nothing. I keep telling you."

"I don't believe you. In fact, unless I get an answer from you tonight, Larry and I will be talking to Pop tomorrow, and he won't take no for an answer. You don't want to end up in the Nursing Home do you?"

"You wouldn't!"

"We would. How do you think he would feel about you wandering in the park late at night?"

"You 've been spying on me too?."

"Larry has been keeping a protective eye on you. Not the same thing. I'm still waiting for an explanation as to why you won't let anyone in your house."

"It's like I said…"

"Don't tell me it's because it's in a mess," Hettie said her voice rising. "Because I don't believe that for one moment and neither does anyone else. What are you hiding in your house?"

Aunt Alice winced. "You'll never believe me."

"Are you protecting Jack? Did he have something to do with Uncle Roscoe's accident?"

"What are you talking about? Of course, he didn't. No one did."

"Who is in your house, Auntie? Why won't you let anyone inside?"

Aunt Alice sagged. Hettie was afraid she was going to have to hold her up.

"I'm afraid of what he might do," she whispered.

"Who, Aunt Alice. Afraid of who?"

"It's whom, Hettie. You of all people should know that."

"Stop trying to change the subject. Who are you talking about?"

"Roscoe."

"What?"

"He's in the house."

Hettie stared at her. "Well, I'm sure you can still feel he's there, Aunt Alice, but..."

"His ghost, Hettie. His ghost is there. I can see him. He died on the Saturday, and he was back on the Tuesday. He's there now on the front porch, waiting for me."

Ceefer groaned.

Chapter 8

Hettie stared at Aunt Alice's house, the empty front porch lit up by the wall sconces either side of the front door.

"You can't see him, can you?" Hettie shook her head. "So, I'm either losing my mind or I'm being haunted by my dead husband's ghost that only I can see. I just keep hoping he'll get bored and go away, or I'll come to my senses."

Hettie pulled her into a hug. "Oh, Aunt Alice."

Hettie's front door opened to reveal Larry, silhouetted in the light from the hall.

"Are you two coming in or are you going to stand out there arguing all night?"

Aunt Alice cast another look at her house. "You'll think I'm only fit for the loony bin anyway," she said, sounding defeated. "It won't matter what Jack thinks."

Larry asked a question with his eyes as he held the door open for a dispirited Aunt Alice. Hettie just shook her head as she followed her aunt inside. In the hall, she helped Ceefer out of his harness. Violet and Gwen were in the kitchen putting slices of roast beef and crispy roast vegetables on the serving platters, while Elly finished setting the table in the dining room.

Violet gave Aunt Alice a hug. "Would you like a glass of wine?" she asked.

"No thanks, Vi."

Violet gave Hettie the same questioning look Hettie had got from Larry.

"This is a little awkward," Hettie said. "We were going to talk after dinner, but Aunt Alice has told me what it is that's been troubling her lately so I think we might be discussing it while we eat."

They all looked at one another as Aunt Alice stood with her arms wrapped around herself staring at the floor. Violet opened a bottle of 2017 Johnny Q cabernet sauvignon that Aunt Alice particularly liked.

"You look a little chilled, Auntie," she said, putting the glass of wine into Aunt Alice's hand. "This will warm you up."

Elly, child free for the evening as Rafe had agreed to babysit, steered Aunt Alice to a seat at the table and put a light throw around her shoulders, before sitting down beside her. Hettie didn't know if she'd ever been so proud of her girls. No one asked what it was Aunt Alice had told her, though she was sure they were all bursting to know.

While Gwen put a platter on the table, Hettie gave a nudge with her head, and Larry and Violet joined her around the corner of the kitchen.

"She's seeing Uncle Roscoe's ghost in her house," she whispered to them.

"Not as bad as we thought, anyway," Larry said.

By the time they all sat down to eat, the message had been passed to Gwen and Elly as well. Hettie thought she probably could have shouted it, as Aunt Alice seemed oblivious to what was going on around her. Violet topped up her aunt's wine glass, the level of which had gone down considerably in a short space of time. As they helped themselves to the food, Hettie noticed Ceefer wasn't around. It wasn't like him to be absent during a meal.

Conversation was a trifle stilted but they managed. Elly told of taking the girls on a play date, and how she should do that more often and keep in touch with her school friends at the same time. Hettie asked Violet how she had enjoyed the Ellington Club with Dan last night.

But it was Gwen who raised the subject they were all wondering how to broach. She and Larry were talking about some Home Opens they had run recently, and how some homeowners had no idea how to present their home in its best light for selling.

"Although sometimes they may have other factors working against them," Gwen said. "Do you remember that house in Appletree Close a couple of years ago, Larry? That really gloomy house."

"I remember your story about it anyway," Larry said.

"You are such a sceptic."

"What was it about, Auntie Gwen?" Elly asked.

"Well, this house was really depressing, even on a bright sunny day. People would come in at the Home Opens, but they wouldn't stay long, and no one made an offer for weeks. It was a nice house too; four bed, two bath, lovely gardens. Then one day this woman came in and looked around and said someone had died there, but they didn't know they were dead, so they hadn't left."

"Spooky," Violet said. "So, what did you do?"

"Well, what anyone would do, I guess. I asked if she could get them to leave, and she said she'd try. She went out into the front garden, and I watched her, like she was speaking to someone, gesturing with her hands. Then she came back in and said she'd done what she could. Well, next time I had the house open for inspection, it was bright and welcoming, and it sold in no time."

"Do you think that's what's happening with Roscoe?" Aunt Alice, who'd said no more than 'yes' or 'no' during the meal, now asked. No one could have missed the hopeful note in her voice.

"It could be," Gwen said. "But why haven't you said anything before, Auntie? Don't you realise how worried we've been about you?"

"Gwen." Hettie considered Gwen's annoyance uncalled for. Gwen waved away Hettie's censure.

"What does he do?" Larry asked, ignoring his wife's comment.

"He's just there," Aunt Alice said. "Just standing there, looking annoyed and – sad."

"Does he say anything?" Elly asked. Aunt Alice shook her head.

"And this is why you haven't been allowing anyone in your home lately?" Larry asked.

"Isn't that enough?"

"Does he frighten you?"

Aunt Alice hesitated, pulling a handkerchief from her sleeve and swiping at her nose. "He makes me jumpy. He just appears right beside me, or he's right there behind me when I turn around. People will think there's something wrong with me. And I don't know what he might do if anyone comes in."

"Has he done something to make you think that?" Hettie asked.

Aunt Alice sighed. "It was probably just too close to the edge of the shelf."

"What was?"

"That little porcelain figurine of the old woman in a chair with her knitting and a cat," Aunt Alice said sadly.

"The pair to the old man polishing a shoe?" Elly asked. Aunt Alice nodded. "What happened to it?"

"Lil called in," Aunt Alice explained, "and there was a crash. Roscoe was standing by the fireplace and there were pieces of the figurine on the hearth. I can't be sure he had anything to do with it falling off, but I can't take the chance. If he can do that, he might hurt someone."

They knew Aunt Alice's first husband, Alan, had given her the pair of figurines in the early days of their marriage. They were only worth a few dollars but had huge sentimental value as a promise of them growing old together. Aunt Alice had treasured them, even more so after Alan's death. They had been on the mantlepiece in her old house and Hettie was sure they were the reason Aunt Alice had insisted on a fireplace in her house at Woody Lake, even if it only held a gas fire.

"Does he follow you when you go out, or is he only in the house?" Hettie asked.

"Well so far, he hasn't followed me anywhere. He's in the front garden and the backyard sometimes."

"Perhaps we need an exorcist," Gwen suggested. Violet immediately pulled out her phone and began tapping away.

"Or someone to clear the house of negative energies," Elly suggested leaning forward. "Megan's mother used to do things like that. Remember, Mum? I told you I took the girls to Megan's on Tuesday. It just reminded me. Vi, try, clearing a house where someone has died."

"Removalists, estate agents," Violet said shaking her head.

Elly frowned. "Cleansing?"

Violet tapped away some more. "Ah, cleansing, getting rid of the negative," she said. "There are heaps here… There's a business that does cleansing... Oh, it's in the US. But there's lots of articles."

"What do you think?" Hettie asked everyone. "Should we try something like that?"

"It can't do any harm, surely," Gwen replied. "What other options do we have?"

Hettie got to her feet. "I'll get my laptop. We can print some of the useful articles." She headed for her study.

"This one says the spirit might be keeping watch on a family member," Violet was saying when Hettie returned. "Perhaps that's what Uncle Roscoe is doing, Auntie. Perhaps he's worried about you."

"Oh dear. I suppose he might be, but I don't know why. He must know I can look after myself. I was doing that before I met him."

Hettie opened the laptop on the kitchen table and Gwen, Violet and Elly gathered around as she replicated Violet's Google search and pulled up the same websites. Soon they were reading over her shoulder. Larry and Aunt Alice remained chatting at the dining table, Larry managing to clean up some of the leftovers at the same time.

"This says people use salt, candles, and smoke from smudge sticks, and herbs, like sage," Gwen read out. "Print that one Hettie. We could try that."

"Someone who suffers a sudden death

might not realise he or she is dead," Elly read. "That's like the story you told us, Auntie Gwen. Wow. This stuff is really interesting. Look here, sometimes a loved one's grief is so strong it binds them to the place." Several pairs of eyes glanced back at Aunt Alice.

"You think Aunt Alice's grief is preventing Roscoe from moving on?" Gwen asked quietly.

"I wouldn't have said their relationship was that strong, but one never really knows about other people's feelings," Hettie replied. "I haven't spoken to Aunt Alice about it yet, but I've made an appointment for her with a grief counsellor."

"It can't hurt," Gwen said.

"So, are we going to do this cleansing?" Violet wanted to know.

"It can't hurt," Gwen said again.

"Unless Uncle Roscoe objects," Elly put in.

"We'll do it together. Safety in numbers," Hettie told them, but she sensed they were all feeling an element of reluctance. They were stepping into the unknown here.

"When will we do it, then?" Elly asked. "I'm free all week."

"The sooner the better," Hettie agreed. "What about Tuesday afternoon? It's sports day, and I don't have classes in the afternoon."

"I'll do some more research tomorrow and talk to Megan," Elly said.

"And I can pop down to Joondalup to shop for what we need," Gwen added, "once Elly gives me a list."

"We're organised then," Hettie said.

When they told Larry and Aunt Alice what they had planned, Larry thought a grief counsellor seemed like the better idea.

"Can they fix an old lady's brain?" Aunt Alice wanted to know.

"Since when did your brain need fixing?" Violet declared. "You're a smart lady. And you're not old. You're not even the oldest person in our family."

Aunt Alice patted Violet's knee. "Thank you dear, but I can't help thinking there must be something wrong with me."

Gwen and the girls helped Hettie clear the table and stack the dishwasher, then Gwen gathered up Larry, and they escorted Elly home. Once they had passed through the gate to Elly's backyard, Hettie switched off the porch light and locked her back door. Not that it would keep out a wandering ghost. She shivered at the thought.

"Would you like to stay over tonight?" Hettie asked her aunt, and was relieved when Aunt Alice said no, she was feeling much better now it had been talked out and they had a plan.

Hettie felt ashamed, but there was the possibility Uncle Roscoe might decide to follow Aunt Alice if she stayed. Hettie wasn't sure she believed in ghosts, but it was one of those things you couldn't be sure about and an open mind on the matter seemed the best idea. She and Violet saw Aunt Alice home to her front door. There was something reassuring about being out on a well-lit street. And of having someone else with you.

Chapter 9

"**W**here's Ceefer?" Violet asked when they were back home. She was refreshing his water bowl. "I haven't seen him since before dinner."

"I haven't either," Hettie replied.

Violet went to look for him but was back in a few minutes looking puzzled. "He's in Elly's room, under the bed. He won't talk to me."

In the few short months Ceefer had been a resident in their home he had been very sociable and very much part of the family. This was odd behaviour for him.

"Perhaps he's not feeling well. He's not throwing up, is he?"

"Yeeuw, no. Not that I saw, anyway."

"I'll have a look at him before I go to bed. If he's not feeling better in the morning, we may need to take him to the vet."

"Okay. Oh, and guess what," Violet said, "there's an exorcist working in Perth. We should call him."

"No, we should not," Hettie said. "Aunt

Alice has agreed to seeing a counsellor, and we're going to try cleansing the house. We'll see how that goes first."

"She's not nuts, Mum."

"No, she's not, but let's deal with the simple straightforward things first."

Violet shrugged. "I've bookmarked the website anyway."

"Good. Just leave it that way for now."

Ceefer was still hiding under Elly's bed when Hettie and Violet checked on him again next morning.

"He hasn't touched his food," Violet said, checking his bowls. "Do you think he's sick?"

Hettie shook her head. "We'll let the vet sort it out, Vi."

The kitchen seemed strangely empty without Ceefer under foot. Not that he ever seemed to get in the way, but his presence was definitely missed. Added to that was the worry about what might be wrong with him, and it was a gloomy breakfast eaten at the kitchen table.

Knowing Ceefer's penchant for getting off his leash, Hettie sent Violet next door to borrow Aunt Alice's cat carrier. Aunt Alice came back with Violet and the carrier, saying she would go to the vet with Hettie, and they could both get off to work on time.

But it was Violet who had to wriggle under the bed to get Ceefer out. No one had said the word 'vet' in his presence but that didn't mean he hadn't heard it. He didn't fight. That wasn't in his nature. His approach was more a hunker down with passive resistance type of objecting, but his displeasure was clear.

"It's for your own good," Hettie told him as she latched the carrier door after getting him inside.

Ceefer didn't answer. His back was turned, his head poked into the corner of what he probably felt was a jail cell.

"I hope you're feeling better soon," Violet told him. "We're going to miss you at the Cafe."

"What's wrong with the poor fellow," Aunt Alice asked as they drove to the Rosny Vet Clinic. "He's certainly under the weather about something."

"That's the thing," Hettie said. "We don't know. He's been like this since last night. He hasn't touched his food and as far as we know he spent the night under the bed in Elly's room."

"Mmm. He hasn't been throwing up at all?"

"Not that we could see," Hettie said though they hadn't checked everywhere in the house. She hoped she wouldn't find any little smelly piles when she went home later.

"Furballs can cause problems sometimes. You've done the right thing, taking him to the vet, anyway Hettie. You'll soon be feeling your usual bright self," she assured Ceefer. He made no comment.

"Are you sure you'll be alright here?" she asked as Aunt Alice took a seat in the vet's waiting room with the carrier at her feet. "I can stay."

Aunt Alice shook her head. "It isn't the first time I've been here, dear, and I'm sure it won't be the last. It's the least I can do."

"You are looking better today. Did you sleep well?"

"Better than I have been, Hettie, thank you. You know how it is. A problem shared is a problem halved."

"That's very true," said Hettie, who now felt she was carrying the other half. "But I'm so pleased you're feeling better."

Hettie rang Aunt Alice at lunch time to check the news about Ceefer and was pleased to hear there was nothing seriously wrong, and she could collect him after work.

"He's moping," James the vet told her. "Has something changed in his life recently?"

Hettie explained the circumstances of their

acquiring Ceefer several months earlier. "But nothing has changed that should have affected him right now. A family member who lived next door died recently, but they had nothing to do with one another."

"Still, he could be picking up on the sadness of family members he is closer to."

Hettie supposed that was possible, or at least picking up on their concern for Aunt Alice. None of them had been particularly close to Roscoe Slater.

"You do know he's not been neutered?"

"I do, but he's an indoor cat and he only goes out on a leash," Hettie explained. No need to mention he could slip off the leash at whim.

"Hmm. Well apart from that, he's in fine shape."

"How old is he, do you think?" Hettie asked. "We've no idea."

"According to his teeth, I'd say he's about three. And if he's in need of anything at all, it's better dental care." The look he gave Hettie suggested she was lacking in not providing this.

"What can I do about that?" she asked instead.

It was the right thing to say, as James waxed lyrical on various products that would take care of the teeth of a dozen cats. "And you need to be careful he isn't getting too many sweet treats. It might feel like you're pampering him, but you aren't doing him any favours if his teeth become loose and painful."

Hettie, appropriately chastened, eventually left the vet's office with Ceefer in his carrier and a bag full of special cat food and dental hygiene products. Ceefer gave her the evil eye when she let him out in the kitchen at home.

"No one likes going to the doctor, Ceef," Hettie told him in her defence. "But we were afraid you might be ill. I'm just so glad you're not." Ceefer sniffed but gave a reluctant 'mruff' in response.

"Moping?" Violet said, when Hettie passed on the vet's diagnosis. She looked at Ceefer who was lying on the sofa, legs tucked under, his back to them facing into the cushions. "Should we get another cat to keep him company, do you think?"

Ceefer's tail whipped back and forth, and he pushed his head further into the cushions.

"Not another cat, I guess," Hettie decided. Unless it was the annoying Aurora.

"Poor boy, what's the matter?" Violet tried to cuddle him, but he voiced his objection and hunkered further under the cushion.

Hettie eyed him dispassionately for a moment. If she had a child in her class behaving this way, she would have said he was sulking. But while she could probably work out what the child's problem might be, she had no idea why Ceefer would be sulking, nor what to do about it.

By late afternoon next day, they were ready for the cleansing of Aunt Alice's house. Elly had read all she could find on the subject. She'd consulted Gwen and they'd decided that a Wiccan approach felt the most comfortable, combined with some processes garnered from other cleansing websites. Both Hettie and Violet agreed with their plan. No one felt comfortable bringing orthodox religion into the situation.

Elly and Gwen shopped and gathered up the items they needed, while Aunt Alice spent the two days vacuuming, dusting, and putting boxes and bags of Roscoe's belongings out on her back patio.

Hettie had offered to help her when she came home at lunchtime, but Aunt Alice didn't want to risk upsetting Roscoe by having someone else in the house. Time enough for that when they did the cleansing. Hettie didn't argue about it. She wasn't looking forward to being in a house with a ghost as it was, but she did wonder how upset he might be already at seeing his belongings cleared out.

At four o'clock they gathered at Aunt Alice's house. Violet had left Tess and the Mrs. B's in charge of the Cafe for the last hour of opening, and Gwen had abandoned their estate agency after lunch so she could help help Elly prepare. Rafe had come home early to care for the girls.

They carried packets of candles, and smudge sticks, and Elly had a hand drawn plan of the house marked with the order of work. Aunt Alice was waiting for them on her garden bench. She looked tired but also more like herself than she'd been of late.

"I'm sorry we couldn't help you today," Hettie said, leaning down for a hug. "It must have been hard for you."

Aunt Alice patted Hettie's shoulder. "I feel as if I can think clearly for the first time in weeks. It's marvelous what a good cleanup can do for your state of mind." She got to her feet. "I've left all the doors and windows open as you said," she told Elly. "Let's do this."

Aunt Alice walked in through the open front door, Elly on her heels, seeming the most eager. Hettie girded herself and followed, Violet and Gwen bringing up the rear. Hettie felt it as soon as she stepped in. She shivered and forced herself not to turn and run. Even with the windows and doors open the house emanated a dark, gloomy atmosphere. Anger seemed to permeate the place, with an underlying sadness.

"This doesn't feel good," Gwen whispered.

"Is Uncle Roscoe here?" Hettie asked also speaking quietly.

"I haven't seen him all day," Aunt Alice replied.

Elly lit a white candle and placed it on the hall table. "We start here," she said. They gathered around and she read out the wording she had created from a Wiccan treatise.

"Protective spirits, we ask a blessing for this cleansing. Please be with us today and add your power to ours. Let all sources of negative energy be lifted away and let all spiritual influences be positive and peaceful."

She lit a smudge stick from the candle and handed Gwen an old-fashioned fan. Gwen waved the fan as Elly held the smudge stick up, sending the smoke wafting around the hall. When Elly was satisfied with the coverage, they moved to the living room. Because this room connected to the dining room and kitchen, Elly placed half a dozen candles around the space before repeating the reading and the smudging.

Hettie wasn't sure about Uncle Roscoe's

ghost, but she thought the humans in the house might have to vacate because of the smoke. She was about to ask Elly if perhaps she was being a little heavy handed with the smudging when a voice called from the hall.

"Alice? Alice, are you here?" Lil appeared waving a hand in front of her face. "What's all this smoke? Is there a fire?"

"No, everything's fine, Lil."

"Oh." Lil stopped when she saw the five of them. She sniffed. "White sage?"

"We're cleansing the house," Hettie told her. "It's common practice when there's been a death."

"It is. You should have mentioned it before. I've had some experience of cleansing," Lil said, which made Hettie wonder how often she'd had trouble with dead people. "But I'd go easy on the smudging, unless you want the fire brigade turning up."

"We've never done this before," Elly told her.

"Obviously." She glanced around the living room. "Do you need some help."

"That's nice of you to offer, Lil, but I think we'd like to do this ourselves," Aunt Alice said.

"Probably as well," Lil said, looking from one to the other. "Uneven numbers work best. Don't forget the lemon wedges." Elly nodded, and Lil turned and left, as abruptly as she'd arrived.

"That's a good neighbour, to come and check on you," Gwen observed.

"What's this about lemon wedges?" Violet asked.

"You leave salt and pieces of lemon in each room for three days to absorb the negative energies," Elly told them. "We've got some."

"We'd best get on," Gwen urged, "or we'll still be doing this after dark."

The sun was sinking by the time they had worked through the bedrooms and bathrooms, being a little more sparing with the smudge stick. The salt and lemon wedges were distributed in each room. There'd been no sign or sound of Uncle Roscoe.

"Do you think the house feels better?" Violet asked.

Everyone stopped to consider for a moment.

"It does feel less gloomy," Gwen said, a little hopefully Hettie thought.

"Time to close the windows and doors," Elly said. They all rushed to help, the swish and clunk of windows sliding shut echoed loudly throughout the house, as if they would keep Uncle Roscoe out.

In the living room, Hettie noticed that the

little figurine of the man, pair to the figure of the woman that Roscoe may have broken, wasn't on the mantlepiece. She wondered if Aunt Alice had put it away for safety.

"I'm making lasagne for dinner tonight," Violet announced. "Who's coming?"

"Rafe was going to do burgers on the barbeque," Elly said. "I told him I wouldn't have the energy to cook tonight, but we'll come. He can do that another night."

Aunt Alice didn't need much convincing to join them at Hettie's house, though she said she would be leaving early, while Gwen said she and Larry were going out. Violet suggested she could sleep over at Aunt Alice's tonight, but Aunt Alice said no, she'd test the house out for herself first. Everyone hoped the house would pass the test.

Chapter 10

It was Friday at last, the final day of Hettie's stint at Rosny Primary, and she knew the kids in her class were arranging a farewell of some sort for her. She had seen the little huddles in the playground that quickly evaporated into giggles when she came into view. Just what were they cooking up?

At least life on Old Dairy Road had been quiet. Aunt Alice hadn't seen Uncle Roscoe since the cleansing. All was good, except for Ceefer, who was still sulking, or moping, or whatever it was. He'd refused to go to the Cafe all week as well. Hettie, in desperation, was beginning to wonder if she should arrange a play date with Janelle Rice's white Persian, Aurora. She would suggest it to Ceefer and see how he reacted.

Hettie looked around her class now with some surprise. The buzzer had sounded for morning recess, and she'd dismissed them, but no one had moved.

"Alright, what's going on?" Her question

was greeted with giggles, while most eyes, she noticed, were on the door. It opened as if on cue, and Ann Potter stood back to let in a woman pushing a trolley laden with cakes and cold drinks. Behind her came Frank with the coffee trolley and the rest of the teaching staff, as well as several mothers and one father.

"Did you arrange all this?" Hettie asked her class, hands on hips.

"Yes, Mrs. P," came the almost shouted response.

"Who baked these lovely cakes?"

"My mum," several voices responded.

"Oh, thank goodness for that," Hettie said, hand on heart. "I was afraid some of you might have had a hand in them." This was greeted by some shouts of laughter but more groans. "Well, come along then. I can't eat them all by myself."

Frank handed her a cup of coffee as her class swarmed around the cake trolley.

"You do realise they are going to be hyped up on sugar for the rest of the day," he said, grinning at her, an evil twinkle in his eye.

"No, they won't," Amy Lord, the mother who had pushed the trolley, told him. "We used stevia."

"You're an angel," Hettie told her.

"Thank you. I have enough trouble dealing

with three kids under normal circumstances without adding sugar to the mix. I can't begin to imagine what a class full would be like." She handed Hettie a plate. "Have a cupcake without the guilt."

"Thank you." Hettie laughed and helped herself to several. Frank did the same. Hettie chatted to the parents who had come along.

"They must enjoy your teaching," the lone father commented, indicating the activity in the room.

"Either that, or they're glad to be rid of me," Hettie replied.

"Could be," he said with a grin.

"Whichever it is, the morning tea was a nice thought," she told him. "I always finish a stint of relief teaching with mixed emotions, I must say. Relief it's over, and sadness at not seeing them all again next week."

"All of them?" he asked, indicating a pair, a boy and girl, arguing further down the room.

"Ah. Excuse me for a moment." Hettie was almost upon the pair before they realised she was there, and their faces showed their dismay.

"What's the problem," she asked, looking at the cheap plastic car, decorated with racing stripe decals, that the boy was holding.

"Nothing, Mrs. P," the girl, Ava, spoke up

first. "Andy's just upset because it broke."

"It's rubbish, look," Andy said. "The door's half orf already. Cory got this really great Jeep. The bonnet comes up and you can see the parts movin' in the ingin. That's what I shoulda got too. It's not fair."

Hettie was at a loss. "Why should you have got the same car as Cory?" she asked. "Where did it come from?" Andy stared at her for a moment and then looked back down at the toy in his hand.

Ava shook her head. "He's making a fuss about nothing, Mrs. P. I've tried to tell him. His prize just hasn't been delivered yet."

"You won something?" she asked Andy. "What did you enter?"

"It's just the competitions in the paper," Ava spoke up quickly. "Lots of us enter them. That's how Cory got his Jeep."

"Oh, I see. Perhaps Cory got first prize, and you got a runner up prize, Andy," she suggested.

"That's prob'ly it," Ava said. She put her arm around Andy's shoulder and drew him away. "Come on, silly, let's get another cupcake."

As Hettie watched them walk away, Ava glanced back over her shoulder, and then quickly looked forward again when she saw

Hettie still had her eyes on them.

Oh dear. Ava was bright, too bright for her own good perhaps. One couldn't say the same for Andy. She thought of the comments in the staffroom about how the kids who were shoplifting weren't spending any money. She had a bad feeling about this. It wasn't the way she'd wanted her time at Rosny Primary to end. Hettie made her way back to the front of the room.

"Refill?" Frank asked, reaching for her cup.

"Thanks. Frank, do you know anything about the competitions the community newspaper runs for kids?"

"Funny you should ask that," he said topping up her cup. "Seems to be a few kids winning some nice prizes lately. The most I ever got was a certificate and five dollars for some puzzle I solved."

Hettie took a sip of coffee. "My girls entered the colouring-in competitions sometimes. I think Elly won twenty-five dollars once, but a certificate and five dollars was about the usual, if they won anything at all."

"Hmm." Frank brushed cupcake crumbs off his shirt. "I suppose with so much news being found on the internet these days newspapers are having to find ways to boost their print readership. They might be trying to breed a new generation of newspaper subscribers, as well as hoping kids will encourage their parents to keep buying the paper version."

"You've actually made sense for a change," Hettie told him. Perhaps she was seeing something that wasn't there, but her instincts told her otherwise. Young Ava was uneasy about something.

Before the buzzer went again for classes to resume, Ann Potter thanked Hettie for stepping in to take the Grade Five class while their class teacher was recovering from her car accident. After the short spurt of clapping was over, the food trolleys and guests dispersed, and Hettie sent her class out for five minutes of fresh air.

She looked around the room at the neat tables that seated six. Pity they didn't still have those old desks with the tops that you open. She wouldn't have minded a quick peak inside right now.

Hettie first task when she got home was to phone Dan Wallace.

"The *Rosny Record* doesn't run the competitions, Mrs. Parke," Dan told her in answer to her query. "None of the newspapers do it themselves. They're run by the Community Newspaper Group."

"Oh, I see. Does that mean all the newspapers have the same kids' page?"

"That's my understanding. Competition entries and anything else – membership of the Koala Club, and stuff – goes to whoever at head office is looking after it."

"So, it's possible then for prizes to be quite substantial?"

"I wouldn't have called them substantial. The kids' page is meant to be another reason for people to open the paper. An awful lot go straight into the recycling bin, or they litter the street when they fall out of letterboxes. Community newspapers survive on getting enough advertising but if the businesses don't feel they're getting a return for their investment, they cancel the advertising. It's a problem that's getting worse with so much news available on the internet."

"That must make your job feel less than secure," Hettie said.

"Which is why I try to investigate local stories. Everyone wants to know what their neighbours are up to." Hettie decided not to comment on that. "But I'll probably end up writing for an online news service eventually."

"Who should I talk to at the Newspaper

Group about the Koala Club?" she asked.

"You'd have to ask reception, but I can give you the office number. Is this something I should know about?"

"Perhaps. We'll have to wait and see."

Her phone pinged with an incoming text containing the phone number she needed. Hettie thanked him and ended the call.

"Are you seeing Dan tonight?" she asked Violet as they cleaned up after dinner that evening.

"No, he's reporting on a council meeting."

"Does he talk about what he's working on?"

"Sometimes." Violet finished stacking the dishwasher and poured half a glass of wine for each of them.

"Mmm. Does he ask questions?" Hettie wanted to know, carrying her wine into the living room and taking a seat on the sofa.

Violet gave her a sharp look as she sat down. "Do you think that's why he's dating me? So he can get the scoop on the Parkes?"

"No, love. He's dating you because you're a lovely smart girl. I also happen to think he's basically a nice fellow. When he isn't digging for dirt, that is. Just be careful."

"I see. So, it's okay for you to use him for information but not okay for him to get information from me, is that what you're saying?"

"I just said you were a smart girl," Hettie replied.

"Oh, for heaven's sake," Violet huffed and switched on the TV, but Hettie could tell she was trying not to smile.

"Mrew?" Ceefer put a paw on Hettie's leg. She put her glass of wine on the coffee table and bent to pick him up. "What is the matter, old fellow? Don't you like living here? Are you missing Miranda?" He bumped his head against her chin and snuggled down but didn't answer. "What if I call Janelle and ask her to bring Aurora over for a play date, Ceefer. Or we could visit her. Would you like that?"

Ceefer buried his head further into Hettie's arm and gave a despairing cry. Had something happened to Aurora that they didn't know about?

On Sunday afternoon, Hettie helped Aunt Alice finish the cleansing of her house. They collected the lemon wedges and salt that had been placed in each room and buried them in the furthest corner of the backyard.

Aunt Alice banged the back of the shovel on the freshly turned earth.

"That's the end of that," she declared. She hadn't seen Uncle Roscoe's ghost since the cleansing on Tuesday. Things were looking up, and she was looking much better Hettie was relieved to see.

Larry was using a wheelbarrow to move Uncle Roscoe's belongings from Aunt Alice's back patio. Some of the boxes and bags were going to a charity shop and Larry was putting those in the back of his SUV, carting them across the backyards to his garage.

"Are these tools to go to the charity shop, too?" Larry asked as he lifted the top of a heavy wooden box.

"I thought they could go to the Men's Shed," Aunt Alice told him, peering at the contents. "Put them in my garage would you, Larry. I'll get in touch with Jim, and they can collect what they want."

Larry hefted the box of tools and Aunt Alice opened the back door of the garage.

"Aaah!" She screamed and stepped back, her hands going to her face.

Larry dumped the box on the ground and quickly stepped around to look into the garage.

He turned a puzzled face to his aunt. "What is it?"

"Roscoe's there," she wailed. "We didn't smudge the garage."

Chapter 11

"**H**e's so angry," Aunt Alice whispered.
"What am I going to do?" She was almost in
tears as she sat at Hettie's kitchen table over a
cup of tea next morning. She had a soggy
shortbread biscuit on the plate beside her,
overly dunked and not eaten.

"What happened exactly?" Hettie asked,
reaching for her aunt's hand across the table.
Ceefer had finally agreed to go with Violet to
the Cafe that morning, and Hettie was thankful
that he might be feeling better. It was easier to
be dealing with one problem at a time.

"Two of my dining chairs went flying
across the room," Aunt Alice told her. "I was
afraid I would get knocked down and not get
up again, so I ran out of the house and came
here. He seems to be really upset about the
cleansing."

"My goodness. Well, you can't go back into
that house, Auntie, not if that's how he's going
to behave. It's dangerous."

"I don't know if I ever want to go back

there, Hettie. It was so nice for those few days after we did the cleansing and smudging. I felt I had my house and my mind back, but now…" She shuddered. "I never thought I'd say this, but perhaps your mother is right, and I need to go live at Sunny Vale."

"Don't give up yet. We'll get the exorcist in and see what he can do about Roscoe. In the meantime, you'll stay here with us."

"I won't say no. It was frightening. I have no idea what he might be capable of. But I will need to get some clothes and things. I ran out of the house with nothing."

Hettie had no wish to confront an angry ghost, especially one she couldn't even see. "I'm not sure it would be a good idea for us to go in there. I'm sure we could provide you with a toothbrush and some clothes for a few days."

"But I have to feed the cats."

Hettie thought quickly. "What if we put some food out on the back patio for them? If we put it by the cat door, they can't miss it."

"It will just encourage rats, Hettie."

"It'll only be for a few days, Auntie. I'll call Vi now and get the details for the exorcist."

She picked up her phone and sent Violet a message. Minutes later she'd received the contact details for a website. She pulled it up in the browser.

"We need to fill in a form," she told Aunt Alice. "I'll have to do it on the laptop."

Hettie filled out the requested details, making sure she only gave an email address for contact and nothing about their location. She had to ask Aunt Alice for some pertinent information on Roscoe's general behaviour before and after the cleansing. Once it was done her finger hovered over the submit button.

"Is there any reason we shouldn't ask this person for help, Aunt Alice?"

"No, dear. I've nothing to hide."

Hettie told herself they were running out of options anyway and pressed the send button.

"**M**um?" Violet called, rushing into the house after work, Ceefer in her arms still in his harness, leash trailing. "What is going on at Aunt Alice's house? Oh." She stared. "Are you going in there?"

"MeerroOW," Ceefer's cry seemed to echo Violet's startled expression.

Hettie put a hand on the yellow hard hat she was wearing. She supposed they did look a little odd. Gwen, Larry and Aunt Alice were all wearing the same.

"Against my better judgement," Hettie said. "It's your uncle's idea. Aunt Alice needs to collect a few things for staying here with us, and Uncle Roscoe's a bit upset but your Uncle Larry seems to think we should be able to handle one elderly ghost."

"A bit upset? The crowd outside think someone's practicing for Halloween."

"What crowd? What are you talking about?"

"What are you talking about?" Violet countered. "You're the one's dressed for trouble. Is that Mum's croquet mallet, Uncle Larry?" Hettie was keeping her new croquet mallet at home after what had happened to the last one.

"Just a precaution," Larry said.

"I doubt it would make much impression on a ghost," was Violet's opinion.

"It might deflect a flying chair," Gwen commented. Hettie began to worry about her mallet. She didn't want another one damaged.

"What was this about a crowd?" Hettie asked again.

"The crowd that's outside looking at what's happening at Aunt Alice's house." Violet told her. "Haven't you looked outside recently?"

"What are you talking about?" Hettie said

going to the front window and peering out. "Oh my. What is going on?"

Hettie counted a dozen people on the footpath and several more at the edge of the park. A man and a woman walking a dog joined the sightseers. Light seemed to be playing across their faces.

"What's going on there, Vi?" Gwen asked as she and Larry joined Hettie at the window. "We can't see Aunt Alice's house from here."

"Um, lightning? Perhaps thunder?" As if to confirm, a low, ominous rumble followed her words.

"Is that coming from my house?" Aunt Alice asked, looking out at the clear blue sky.

"Um, yeah."

Hettie watched the light play over the people outside as a louder rumble reached their ears.

"Someone's going to call the police if that keeps up," she said swinging away from the window. "How are we going to explain about a ghost?"

"We'd better get over there and sort it out," Larry said. "And I thought a cat that understands what we say was weird enough."

"Con, then," Hettie urged as she headed for the back door.

"Do you have another hard hat?" Violet

asked, following them.

"No," Gwen told her, as Hettie said, "You can't come, Vi."

"I am coming." She put Ceefer on the floor.

"No, wait. The police might turn up before we get back. Probably Sergeant Higgins. Keep him talking while we settle Uncle Roscoe." If they could. Just how bad was it?

"What do I tell him?" Violet called, but Hettie was off, her fellow ghostbusters already out of sight.

Nothing prepared Hettie for what she saw when she rushed into Aunt Alice's backyard. The house was shimmering. The walls no longer seemed perfectly straight or solid. Lightning flashed in the windows. Aunt Alice had unlocked the back door and disappeared inside, as had Larry. Gwen was just stepping in when Hettie caught her up. She could hear Aunt Alice calling to Uncle Roscoe. Thunder rolled overhead echoing through the house. Hettie put both hands over her ears, but Gwen grabbed her arm as they crept forward, and Hettie found it was hardly worth covering just one ear.

They both paused in the hallway. Aunt Alice was standing just inside the living room, Larry beside her, both hands on Hettie's mallet at the ready. The furniture still had all its legs on the floor, for the moment anyway. Lightning flashed in the room and thunder crashed again, filling the whole house with sound. Hettie smelt a whiff of smoke and hoped the lightning hadn't caught something alight.

"Keep the mallet low, Larry," she called between thunder rolls. You didn't play croquet in a thunderstorm.

Through the noise of the thunder and the flashes of light, they could hear Aunt Alice speaking to Uncle Roscoe but could only hear the occasional word between the thunder. Hettie thought she was being incredibly brave. Clearly, she didn't believe Uncle Roscoe would hurt her. Not on purpose anyway. His behaviour seemed to be more in the way of a temper tantrum, something to draw attention. Hettie wondered if he didn't have a choice about moving on. That would be enough to make any ghost angry. If only they knew what was keeping him here.

A flash of lightning sizzled the edge of the hall rug and Gwen yelped. Then the doorbell chimed, and the thunder rolled again.

Aunt Alice raised her voice. "That will be the police, Roscoe," she shouted. "They'll arrest me for causing a disturbance if you keep this up. Do you want me sent to jail? I don't know why you're still here. Do you think I can't manage without you? I do miss you, you must know that, but I wouldn't keep you here. I have my family."

A deafening crash had Hettie's ears ringing as if her eardrums would burst. If they hadn't been sure how Uncle Roscoe felt about the Parkes before, they certainly knew now.

"If I'm keeping you here, Roscoe, you have my permission to leave. You must know you're dead. I'm terribly sorry for being angry at you for cleaning out the gutters."

The next flash of lightning was more subdued but the pounding on the door and the shouts of 'Police' were not.

"I hope he doesn't try to break in," Gwen whispered.

"We shouldn't be here if he does," Hettie whispered back. "I'm not sure how we would explain this."

"And I'm sorry about the smudging," Aunt Alice was saying now. "But we thought you might need help to leave." A low distant roll of thunder and a brief flash greeted her words.

"We need to leave, now," Hettie whispered urgently as the pounding on the front door increased. She didn't know if reinforcements had been called. "Larry, Aunt Alice. We need to go."

"You need to rest now," Aunt Alice said. "I'm going to stay at Hettie's tonight, and we'll be discussing what to do. We'll figure something out. Stay calm dear, please. I'll see you tomorrow."

Larry remained by the living room door, mallet in hand, as Aunt Alice cast one last look back before slipping down the hallway after Hettie and Gwen. Larry brought up the rear like some armed warrior defending the retreat. A flash of lightning lit their way, but the force had gone out of the demonstration.

They were greeted at Hettie's back door by the sound of Johnny Farnham's *The Voice* at high volume. Violet met them looking immensely relieved.

"We need to hide these hats," Hettie said, pulling off her own hard hat and grabbing up the others. "Pour some wine and get some food out. Stuart will be here any minute now that he's not getting an answer next door."

She hurried to her bedroom, putting the hats on the top shelf of her walk-in wardrobe as if they had been there for years.

"That was clever of you to have the music on," Larry was saying to Violet when Hettie returned to the living room. Her doorbell chimed. "I'll get it." He headed for the hall with a beer in his hand.

When Sergeant Higgins entered, he found Aunt Alice on the sofa beside Violet, wine glass in hand. Ceefer was on Violet's lap, and in the kitchen Gwen and Hettie were looking busy.

Larry casually turned down the volume of the music. "That song is always best listened to at volume, isn't it?" he said. Stuart Higgins didn't comment. "What can we do for you, Sergeant?"

"Am I to believe none of you were aware of the ruckus next door at Mrs. Slater's house?" Stuart asked.

"What ruckus was that?" Hettie asked. "Between Johnny Farnham and the thunderstorm, we didn't hear anything else." She was drying her hands on a tea towel and continued to hold it. If she didn't do something with her hands, he might see they were shaking. It was a reaction to what they had just experienced, the adrenalin surge, but he might think – correctly – she had something to hide if he saw them.

Stuart eyed her coolly. "Thunder and lightning in the house next door. Enough to draw a crowd."

"Lightning as well?" Larry said, glancing toward the window where the fading light still showed a clear sky.

"Did you say IN the house?" Hettie asked.

"Merrow."

"Oh, you haven't had your dinner," Violet said and took Ceefer into the kitchen where she proceeded to open a tin of cat food and fill his bowl.

"Never stops eating that fellow," Larry commented.

Stuart's expression warned Hettie they were doing too good a job of pretending they didn't know anything. Too relaxed. Not curious enough about what he claimed had been going on. If they were a television show the viewers would be groaning at the bad acting. The tension in the room seemed to stretch out.

"I have a confession to make," Aunt Alice said.

Chapter 12

"**A**unt Alice…" Larry and Hettie both spoke at once. A confession? Aunt Alice held up her hand.

"Yes, yes, I know not everyone believes in ghosts, but I'm sure the Sergeant will understand. In his line of work he must have come across cases where things weren't as straightforward as they first appeared."

"Ghosts?" Stuart's eyebrows rose to his hairline. His gaze swept them. If anything, it was even more suspicious.

"We don't have the answer to everything, Sergeant. Please sit down." She indicated the other armchair. "You'll have to excuse my family. They are only trying to protect me."

"I can well believe that Mrs. Slater," he said heavily. "A confession, you said."

Hettie felt rooted to the spot. Her stomach churned. What was Aunt Alice going to confess to? Had Uncle Roscoe's behaviour stirred her to tell them what really happened that Saturday morning? Gwen stood nearby, her fingers looking about to snap the stem of her wine glass.

"My husband may be dead and buried," Aunt Alice began, when Stuart was seated, notebook in hand. "But his ghost still walks and occupies our house."

"I…see."

Aunt Alice nodded. "We tried a cleansing to send him to wherever he's supposed to go, but he hid in the garage. This morning he tried throwing chairs at me. I don't think he really wanted to hurt me, but he's clearly upset about… about dying, I suppose. It would be just like him. He wasn't one to take misfortune lying down. He ranted and raved about the way life had treated him. He won't have changed just because he died. What you saw tonight was just another example of that, I guess."

"This… ghost… created thunder and lightning in your house," Stuart repeated. "Is that what you're saying?"

"It was rather spectacular, wasn't it?" Aunt Alice replied. "I managed to calm him down, but I don't know how long that will last or what we can do if he continues to behave this way. How do you send someone on their way, Sergeant? You must have more experience with death in your line of work."

"You can see this ghost, can you?"

"Yes, of course, it's how I know it's Roscoe."

"Has anyone else seen this ghost?" he asked, looking around the room. Four heads shook in unison.

"I see." Stuart tucked his notebook back in his top pocket, having not written a word, and got to his feet. "I feel I should warn you about playing fast and loose with the law," he said, taking a long look at each of them, including Aunt Alice. "You need to remember that no one, and I mean no one, is above the law. I suggest you consider that carefully. Have a good evening." He stalked out.

Hettie and Larry exchanged a look and dashed after him. Outside, the crowd had all but dispersed, and there wasn't a sound from Aunt Alice's house.

"Fast and loose with the law?" Hettie challenged. "What are you accusing us of doing, Stuart?"

Stuart gave her a cool look. "You tried denying you knew what was going on next door for a start."

Hettie was suitably embarrassed. "I'm sorry about that, but ghosts aren't exactly a police matter, are they? And we are a bit out of our depth."

"Oh, I think you know exactly what you're

doing, Hettie. Mrs. Slater said it herself. You're protecting her. I imagine it wouldn't be all that difficult to get a video of thunder and lightning. Play it at high volume, add some strobe lights or something to enhance the effect."

"You think we set this up?" Larry asked.

"It would be one way to protect an old lady, wouldn't it?" Stuart said, turning to him. "Have her believe she isn't quite sane and anything untoward she might have done is just in her imagination. I imagine, after some time, if she ever changes her story about what happened to her husband, no one will believe anything she says."

"You can't be serious," Hettie responded. "Aunt Alice is as sane as anyone of us."

"I think that's what the Sergeant was implying, Sis."

"Oh."

"This isn't over," Stuart said and marched off to his police car parked in Aunt Alice's driveway. A low rumble from the house saw Stuart's step falter for a moment, before he reached his car and drove off. Rather quickly, Hettie thought.

"That is one very suspicious police officer," Larry commented. "Hello. Who have we got here?"

Three figures had appeared from the other side of Lil's house and were now heading their way. The streetlights showed them to be Eddie, Frank and Gloria.

"What in heaven was all that?" Eddie asked, his eyes round.

"Uncle Roscoe," Hettie told them, as they came inside. "He's a bit upset."

"A bit!"

"Was that Sergeant Higgins?" Frank asked.

"It was. A very unhappy and suspicious Sergeant Higgins I'm afraid."

In the living room family members greeted one another. As drinks were handed around, the Parkes updated the Garcias on what had just gone down.

"I've made things worse," Aunt Alice said. "I could see he didn't believe us when we pretended not to know what was happening at my house, but I thought telling the truth might satisfy him."

Hettie shook her head. "Stuart's always been suspicious of what happened to Uncle Roscoe. We've just confirmed it with what he sees as our attempt to protect you."

"What a mess," Eddie said. "What do we do now?"

Gloria was the only one with an answer to that. "You need an exorcist, Alice. You need to get rid of that malignant presence in your house."

"Malignant?" Aunt Alice was affronted. "That's my husband, Gloria, if you don't mind."

Gloria leant forward in her chair, pointing her finger at Alice. "He's bad news. He needs to be sent on his way. He doesn't belong in this realm anymore."

"We've already asked for help from an exorcist, Gloria," Hettie said, as Aunt Alice looked to be about to tell Gloria what she thought of her ideas. "We're just waiting on a reply."

"Good, good." Gloria sat back looking satisfied.

"An exorcist," Eddie said in disgust.

"Any better idea?" Larry asked.

"You could get rid of that black cat," Gloria said, her voice rising as Ceefer leapt up onto the sofa between Hettie and Aunt Alice.

"Mroow?"

Gloria crossed her forefingers in front of her.

"Let's not argue among ourselves about this," Hettie put in quickly, putting a protective hand on Ceefer.

"I think we need to go," Frank said getting to his feet. "Can we walk you home, Aunt Alice?"

"No, thank you Frank," Aunt Alice said with a sharp glance at Gloria. "I'll be staying here with Hettie for a few days."

"I'll call in and see you tomorrow, Alice," Eddie said. Aunt Alice just nodded.

"These things only started happening since that cat arrived," Gloria was heard saying as her brother and nephew escorted her out, Larry in their wake to see them off.

So on top of everything else there was now dissension in the family. Hettie wondered if it could get any worse.

"**M**um, Ceefer's run away," Violet wailed mid-way through the following morning.

"What?" Hettie moved the phone a little further from her ear. She was in the supermarket, trying to decide if Ceefer would accept the generic brand of tuna in place of the more expensive choice. It probably tasted the same, but he might have other ideas if he saw the can.

"He snuck out the door when some people came in for lunch," Violet went on. "Mrs. Bronson saw him. They both ran out after him, but he disappeared."

"He's never done that before, has he?"

"No, of course not. Who should we call? The police? The RSPCA?"

The 'Ghostbusters' song played in Hettie's head for one mad moment. "I don't suppose he was wearing his harness?" she managed to say.

"No, of course not. He doesn't wear it inside."

Which meant he was just another black cat like all other black cats. Would she even be able to recognise Ceefer among a group of black cats? She couldn't see the aura that Janelle claimed he had.

"He's probably seen a female cat in the garden and gone out to get acquainted," she said. "He'll be back when he gets hungry."

She could only hope anyway. It was clear he hadn't been happy this past week. Perhaps he really was missing his old life, whatever that had been. She realised how little they knew of him. Why did Ian leave Ceefer with Violet at the Cafe? Had he run away from other places where he'd been left?

She heard voices in the background and Violet responding but couldn't catch the words.

"Is he back already? Vi?"

"Mum," she said her voice loud again, "Aunt Alice and the Mrs. B's are organising a search party. I'll let you know what happens."

Hettie doubted the search party would be successful. Ceefer could disappear into backyards and laneways, and under bushes. She didn't want to think of him crossing busy roads. She put the can of tuna back on the shelf. There was no need for it now.

Despite her belief it was a waste of time, Hettie spent several hours scouring the parks along the river, peering into trees and getting hot and dishevelled. But there was no sign of a black cat. She hadn't really expected there would be, but she'd had to try.

She finally headed for home. Parked outside her house was a battered green Volkswagen. It probably belonged to someone taking a walk in the park. But there, sitting on her front porch like a pair of bookends, was a large, sleek black cat and a smaller, fluffy white one.

"Ceefer." Her first coherent thought was that Ceefer had catnapped Aurora, but then a plump woman, swathed in layers of bright floaty fabrics, stood up from the garden bench.

"Where did you find Ceefer?" Hettie asked.

Janelle Rice huffed. Nothing had changed

there then. "I didn't," she said. "He found me. What's all the fuss about?"

Hettie frowned at Ceefer and then looked at Aurora. "I don't know. Perhaps he wanted company." And perhaps she should have arranged a few more play dates and avoided all this stress and fuss.

"He wouldn't have insisted on me coming here if that's all it was," Janelle said still grumpy.

"MerroOW."

"He insisted?" Janelle and the two cats just looked at her. "Well, I guess you'd better come in."

Hettie unlocked her door and led the way to the kitchen, Janelle and the cats following. She put the kettle on as Ceefer sniffed at his bowl.

"I suppose you're hungry after all that exercise," she said to him. It was a ten-minute drive to Janelle's house on the other side of Woody Lake. Not a small journey for a cat on four paws.

"I have fed him," Janelle said.

"It would seem he never stops eating," Hettie replied and emptied the last can of tuna into his bowl. She would have to go shopping again later. "Excuse me a moment," she said pulling out her phone. "I need to make a call.

There's a search party out looking for a certain black cat." She heard Violet's phone ring. "Hello, Vi. Ceefer's home."

After Violet had stopped jumping for joy, she said she would phone the searchers and tell them the good news. Hettie thought she heard a cheer from inside the Cafe.

"It sounds as if they missed you at the Cafe, Ceef," she told him.

The kettle boiled. She made coffee for herself and a herbal tea for Janelle, using a teabag she provided herself. She always brought her own, Janelle explained, as no one seemed to have the tea she liked. Hettie thought if she was going to be fussy about what she drank it was the least she could do, rather than make a person feel they were lacking hospitality when they couldn't provide it.

"Why are you here?" Hettie asked.

"I'd think that was something you need to tell me," Janelle replied.

Hettie looked at Ceefer, who had finished eating and was now sitting watching them. Aurora had made herself comfortable on the sofa. This must be serious if the two cats weren't creating mayhem as usual.

Hettie took a stab at an answer. "What do you know about exorcising a ghost?"

"Not a lot." Hettie frowned. "What's been

happening?"

Hettie explained the situation as briefly as possible. It soon became clear that Janelle wasn't immediately eager to help.

"She's probably just projecting," she told Hettie, referring to Aunt Alice. "Overcome with guilt because she told him not to get up on that ladder, and then ignored him when he did, and he fell. Not at all unusual to be carrying guilt for that."

"Perhaps. But how do you explain the demonstration last night? There were four of us in the house and a crowd watching from outside. Not to mention a police officer. Seemed pretty darn real at the time."

Janelle glared and then looked down at her cup. "So, what do you want to know?" she asked.

Chapter 13

"I think we would like to know why he's here. And then, how to get him to leave."

"I can do the first thing. Once you know why, you'll be able to deal with the rest yourself."

Hettie felt that helping him leave might depend on the answer to why he was here. Did Roscoe believe Aunt Alice was responsible for his accident? Did he have to see her arrested before he would leave? Hettie had to wonder if breaking his wife's little old lady figurine had been a message. She fervently hoped not.

"He doesn't talk to Aunt Alice, though," she told Janelle.

"Ghosts don't talk, in my experience. I feel what they have to say."

"I see," Hettie said, although she didn't.

"Well? I don't have all day. Where do we find him?"

"He's next door. Will you be able to see him?"

"Aurora will. She's my conduit."

"Could Ceefer have done this then?" Hettie asked, looking at him, watching and listening. Ceefer put a paw across his eyes.

Janelle gave a sharp laugh. "No. He can't, but she can." As if that was a one-up on Ceefer. Had that been the reason for the sulking? Because Aurora could do something he couldn't?

"But that's why Miranda wanted them to get together," Janelle explained. "She hoped they might have kittens with a combination of their talents. That would be some awesome cat."

So, Aurora's talent was as a ghost conduit. Or one of her talents, anyway. Hettie wasn't altogether sure just what Ceefer's talents were. She was certain he understood what people were saying, and he did have an uncanny knack for finding people she needed to talk to.

Her front door opened, and Violet rushed in. She wasn't alone. Not only was Aunt Alice with her, but both the Mrs. B's as well. They piled into the kitchen and made a fuss of Ceefer and Aurora, who both lapped up the attention.

"This is exciting," Mrs. Bronson said as they trooped out front and across to Aunt Alice's house. Violet was carrying Ceefer, and Janelle had Aurora in her arms. Before they reached Aunt Alice's front porch, Aurora gave an eldritch shriek.

The hair stood up on Hettie's arms at the sound. Aurora stiffened, fur on end. She let out another shriek, causing several of those present to wince, Hettie included.

"I take it she can see something," Hettie said through gritted teeth.

"Roscoe's just – appeared in the garden," Aunt Alice said hoarsely. "Can the cat really see him?" she asked, turning to Janelle who was soothing Aurora. Janelle nodded. "Oh, thank goodness. I'm not going mad then."

"Is she alright?" Mrs. Bronson asked. "She seems rather upset."

"She had a bad experience with a ghost once," Janelle replied. "Turned out he'd been a wolf in a previous life. It cost her one of her nine lives. Cats don't forget things like that, you know. She'll calm down in a moment once she's sussed him out."

"Merrow," Ceefer said, fur on end and looking ready to jump to her defence.

Hettie blinked. This was way out of her comfort zone.

"You need to be quiet," Janelle ordered now. "Otherwise, I won't hear him, and I only get one chance."

Everyone stepped back to the edge of Aunt

Alice's garden as Janelle faced Roscoe, or in the direction where Aunt Alice had said Roscoe was standing anyway. She held out one hand, palm up. Her head was up and back a little. Hettie couldn't see her face but imagined her eyes were closed. A silence of sorts descended on the group. The tweeting and calling of birds in the park and the hum of traffic in the distance seemed clearer than usual. Time seemed to stand still until with a sigh, Janelle's arm dropped to her side and her body sagged.

Aunt Alice reached her first, taking her arm. She helped Janelle to the garden bench. The woman looked exhausted.

"Tea," she said. "I need a cup of peppermint tea. And something to eat."

Back in the kitchen, Hettie quickly brewed a cup of peppermint tea from a tea bag Janelle dug out of her bag. Everyone else had coffee or English Breakfast tea, which was the only tea Hettie ever had. Violet produced lemon drizzle cupcakes and Janelle polished off three in quick succession, while Ceefer and Aurora refreshed themselves from Ceefer's water bowl and finished the rest of the tuna. Hettie thought both cats deserved it. What a performance. Which thought made her wonder.

She was impatient to know what Janelle

139

was going to tell them now. The woman seemed to be enjoying the attention from Aunt Alice and the Mrs. B's, but Hettie found herself suddenly filled with doubts. Had Janelle's initial reluctance to be involved been just an act? Were they about to be hit with a request for money? A greasing of the palm? Perhaps she used Ceefer and Aurora to lure in unsuspecting victims. If that was so, she was certainly clever, and happy to play a long game. But then the Parkes might be worth that, in Janelle's mind anyway.

"Feeling better?" Hettie asked.

Janelle certainly looked refreshed. "I am, thank you," Janelle said, "but I will be having a nap when I go home."

"So, what did Roscoe tell you?" Aunt Alice asked, leaning forward.

"He didn't tell me anything," Janelle said, with an emphasis on the tell. "I see what he experienced," she hastened to say as Aunt Alice's face fell.

"And what was that?" Hettie asked.

"He was on the ladder, scraping leaves into a bucket. He climbed down and emptied the bucket into the wheelbarrow. Twice he did that before he moved the ladder."

"We get a lot of leaves blowing in from the park," Aunt Alice commented.

Janelle nodded. "He was annoyed about that. So much work, up and down. Someone should have told him to just tip the bucket into the wheelbarrow from up on the ladder, but I got the impression he didn't take to being told anything."

Aunt Alice nodded. "You're right about that." Hettie frowned. Had Janelle ever tipped a bucket of leaves from a height? She could picture them drifting and floating over the lawn and very few landing in the wheelbarrow. She didn't think Janelle was very practical, but she did tell a good story, and there was nothing of the mercurial behaviour she had come to associate with the woman.

"There was the sound of a vacuum cleaner," Janelle continued, "and a dog barked nearby. Roscoe was annoyed about that too."

"Howie, next door," Aunt Alice.

"But then the ladder jerked, like it was hit by something." Aunt Alice gasped. "It slipped against the wall. He grabbed for the gutter to steady himself, but the gutter broke away and he fell. There was a red flash and – nothing."

Gasps from the rest of the listeners echoed Aunt Alice.

"Are you saying someone pushed the ladder?" Hettie asked.

"Pushed, bumped. It's what he believes.

But he didn't see anything. He didn't look down. He was concentrating on saving himself from falling."

"Did he call out?" Aunt Alice asked faintly.

"He called out your name, Alice."

That was what the neighbour at the back had heard, according to Stuart. Hettie couldn't remember if she had mentioned it. Janelle could be setting up an attempt at extortion, creating the suspicion that Aunt Alice had pushed the ladder. She wouldn't know it was a bit late for that.

"To put it simply, Roscoe Slater wants to know what happened to him," Janelle said flatly. "Unfinished business."

"But the police have already investigated," Aunt Alice said.

"Well, they can't have done a very good job then." She yawned. "I need to go." She got to her feet and collected Aurora from the sofa.

"Mrew?" Ceefer raised his head.

"You might want to bring Ceefer over for a play date once in a while," she said to Hettie, and left without a backward glance.

What a day and it still wasn't even time for dinner. Hettie had so much to tell Gwen and Larry. She could get Chinese food delivered tonight. That would make life simple. She picked up her phone to call Gwen.

"Sorry, no can do," Gwen said. "We're having dinner with our salespeople tonight. We'll be back early enough for a nightcap, if that suits?"

Hettie's mind was bursting, and she needed to unload. "What about now? Do you have fifteen minutes? I have a lot to tell."

"Okay. But it better be worth it. I still need to shower and put myself back together, and I don't need Larry making like Ayrton Senna on the way."

Considering the famous racing car driver's untimely end, Hettie thought that was probably a good idea. She told Violet she was popping over to Larry's and dashed out, but not before she heard her tell Ceefer, "Mum can't wait to spill the beans." She didn't hear Ceefer's response.

She gave the gate to Elly's backyard a good shove as she opened it. The hinges had been getting stiff lately. Instead of barely moving, the gate flew open and banged against the fence, startling not only her, but Rafe, who was watching Jazmin on the trampoline.

"Sorry about that," Hettie said, retrieving the gate and closing it gently. There was a small dent in the fence where it had hit. "I didn't know you'd oiled the hinges."

"I didn't oil it," Rafe confessed. "It must have been Larry."

"Oh, well, I'm just passing through right now, Rafe."

"Look at me, Nan," Jazmin shouted, seemingly unfazed by the sudden noise, as she executed a sit-down-stand-up bounce.

"Wonderful," Hettie told her. "What a clever girl you are."

"Tell Larry thanks," Rafe said. "For oiling the gate, I mean. I might forget next time I see him."

"I will. If I don't forget," she replied with a grin. She opened the gate to Larry's backyard with more care. It moved smoothly as well.

It took her ten minutes non-stop to relay the day's events to Gwen and Larry. When she finished, she took her first sip from the half glass of white wine Larry had poured for her.

"That must have been something to see," Gwen said. "And Ceefer came through once again."

"Eventually," Hettie said.

Larry gave his head an upward tilt and tsked. "You make far too much of that cat, both of you."

"You're the one who's always talking to him mano a mano," Gwen scoffed. "Anyway," she said, "I find it very telling that Janelle said Roscoe could hear the vacuum cleaner before he fell. Unless you told her Aunt Alice had said she was vacuuming?" she added.

Hettie looked a little abashed. "Not sure. Might have." She had told Janelle rather a lot of what had happened.

"That's how they work, those so-called mediums and fortune tellers. They get information from you and then repeat it back, as if it came from the person you're trying to contact, or if it's a genuine prediction for your future."

Hettie knew all that and was irritated at Gwen for pointing it out, especially if she was right. Had she been so surprised at Janelle's appearance on her doorstep, and her hope of a solution to the ghost problem, that she'd revealed too much?

"I did doubt her," Hettie said now. "I kept expecting a demand for money. It sounded like she was setting up Aunt Alice as the only person who could have done it."

"She might still ask for something to keep quiet," Gwen said.

Hettie put down her now empty glass and got to her feet. "Well, I won't hold you up any longer." The back door squeaked as she opened it.

"Oh, that reminds me," she said over her shoulder. "Rafe said to thank you for oiling their gate."

"I didn't oil their gate," Larry replied.

"He hasn't oiled the hinges on the back door either," Gwen called as she headed for the bedroom.

"Well, that's obvious," Hettie answered back. If Gwen thought she could get away with telling her she'd walked into Janelle's trap she could think again. "It felt like your gate had been oiled recently too," she told Larry.

He shrugged. "It was probably our Mick." They shared a Mick's Mowing contractor who did all their back lawns at the same time.

Back home, Hettie opened the calendar on her phone. Because she'd been working, she'd lost track of when the lawns had been mown last. According to the schedule she had, their Mick's last visit had been the Thursday two days before Uncle Roscoe's accident. That meant they were due to mow again this week.

Hettie tried to remember when she'd last used the gates. Oh, yes. Jazmin had wanted to say goodnight one evening and Elly had brought the girls over. She'd gone back with Elly to read them a story and tuck them in. That must have been the Thursday after they'd done the cleansing on Aunt Alice's house, when life had felt normal for a short while.

But what it meant was that Mick's Mowing weren't the ones who'd oiled their gate hinges.

Chapter 14

Ceefer didn't want to go to the Cafe with Violet on Wednesday.

"I hope you're not expecting Aurora to come for another visit," Hettie told him. Ceefer just huffed.

Aunt Alice had plans for the day as well. "I'm going to talk to Roscoe again," she told Hettie. "I thought I might try to convince him his fall off the ladder really was an accident as no one could have been there."

"You don't think he might get upset because you don't believe him about the ladder being bumped?"

Aunt Alice put her hands out in an, 'I've no idea' gesture. "I need to do something Hettie. This can't go on. I mean, it's possible one side of the ladder slipped into a soft patch of ground, isn't it? That would cause a jolt, and he had just moved it, according to Janelle."

"That's a reasonable explanation, Auntie. Do you want me to come with you and add my support?"

"That's kind of you dear, but I think it's better if I do it by myself. I won't stay long, just long enough to give him something to think about. I might go to Elly's for a while after that. She has work to do, and Jazmin still only has kindergarten two days a week. Oh, and I've talked to Jack, did I tell you? About the police."

Hettie felt relieved to hear that. "What did he have to say?"

"Hang tight and stick to your story, he said. I told him that's what I've been doing."

Hettie agreed it was the only sensible approach. And if Aunt Alice couldn't convince Roscoe that the ladder had just slipped and not been bumped by someone, they would just have to wait until they heard back from the exorcist. She hoped a visit from that person wouldn't set Uncle Roscoe off again, but if it did they would have someone there who supposedly knew what to do about it. With nothing else pressing, Hettie thought it was time she followed up on her theory regarding the argument she witnessed between her two former pupils.

She picked up her phone, intending to call the number Dan had given her and talk to the person who ran the Koala Club children's page.

"Merroooow." Ceefer was at her feet, his paw on her leg.

"What's the matter," she said, bending down to rub his head. He stretched up and grasped at her phone with his paws. "Do you want to call someone?"

For answer, he raced to the hall, and she heard several thumps before he returned dragging his harness.

"MerrooOOW."

"We're going out?" She looked at her phone and back at Ceefer. "We're going to visit them instead of phoning, aren't we?"

"Mruff."

"Well, I suppose that makes sense. It's easy to fob people off over the phone." She opened the browser on her phone instead.

"Merreww." He was at her feet again, paw on her leg.

"I need to find their address, Ceef. I'm not phoning them, alright?"

"Mruff." The paw was removed.

"Apology accepted." She searched online for the Community Newspaper Group and found the address, checking that the number Dan had given her matched the one on their website. "Leederville." She told Ceefer. "We're going to Leederville."

Parking would be at a premium in the inner-city suburb, so it made sense to take the train, especially as Leederville was the second to last station heading into the city, making it a direct connection. With Ceefer on his leash, Hettie crossed the footbridge over the Cygnet River and took the path to the right, along the river to the Rosny Station. Ceefer received the usual attention he got when he walked in his harness. Hettie smiled and nodded and tried to remember what it was like to go anywhere incognito.

Once they'd left the station at Leederville it was only a matter of minutes before they were crossing Oxford Street to the two-storey building on the corner of Newcastle Street. The upper floor housed the Community Newspapers' administration offices. Hettie opened the street door and carried Ceefer up the stairs. She put him down again on the landing, in front of a glass door marked with the words 'Community Newspaper Group.'

The receptionist's eyes widened at the sight of Ceefer strutting confidently in, but she became all business when Hettie said she wanted to see the person who managed the children's pages. She directed Hettie to take a seat while she made a call. A minute or two later, a plump, older woman appeared from a glassed-in cubicle at the far end of the long room, which was lined with similar cubicles down both sides.

She walked up the reception area to meet Hettie and introduced herself as Christine Selfridge. She was grey-haired and in her sixties and wore a blue sweater sporting the Koala Club logo. Hettie thought she was the stereotype of a grandmother with the very grandmotherly job of looking after a children's club.

Hettie introduced herself. "Thank you for seeing me. I wanted to talk to you about the prizes you award for the competitions in your children's pages."

Christine frowned. "I don't know what you expect," she said, launching right in. "I have a ten dollar limit you know, except for the quarterly competition when I can spend twenty-five. How many toys do you think I can find at those prices? Tell me that?"

Hettie saw the receptionist's eyes grow rounder.

"Not many of any quality, I would expect," she said reasonably, having bought Christmas and birthday presents for Rosa and Jazmin. Ten dollars didn't buy much.

"That's right," Christine said, sounding a little less sure of herself.

"Would it be possible to see what prizes you do have?"

Christine crossed her arms on her chest.

"Why?"

Hettie glanced at the receptionist who was making no secret of listening to them. "Perhaps I'm not explaining myself properly. Do you have an office where we could talk? Or is there someone else I should be speaking to?"

"No, no," Christine said, a trifle too quickly. "We can talk in my office."

Hettie and Ceefer followed her down the centre of the room, getting looks from most of the people working in their cubicles as they passed. Christine's cubicle looked more like a storage cupboard, with a desk pushed against the side wall, its surface untidy with papers. Several of the red plastic cars with racing stripes, like the one young Andy had been complaining about on Friday, sat on one pile of papers.

Along the back wall were shelves and a stack of unopened boxes. Hettie saw the labels for Reflex paper and printer cartridges, as well as an open box containing more plastic cars, these in blue and green as well as red. The green was an ambulance, and the blue a police car, each with the relevant decals.

"I don't imagine this is a fulltime job," Hettie commented. The office space was clearly multi-purpose. There was only one chair and that was in front of the desk, which would have blocked the doorway when in use. Pushed in, it allowed the two of them enough space to stand. Ceefer sat close to Hettie's feet.

"It's only two days a week," Christine said. "I'm retired, really. Put out to pasture when they wanted a younger face at reception. I'm still the one they ask when they want to know something though."

Hettie nodded sympathetically. "You've worked here for some time then?"

"Twenty years. So, what is it you want?"

"One of the boys in my Grade Five class was talking about the prize he had received for a competition. It was one of those red sports cars you have on your desk. He was expecting a prize similar in quality to what another boy had won. But you mentioned a quarterly competition with a more expensive prize. Perhaps the other boy had won that one, and this boy was mistaken about what he should have got."

Christine shrugged. "Possibly. What was the other prize, do you know?"

"It was described as a metal car, a Jeep, with doors that opened and shut. It must have been battery operated as there was movement in the engine. More than that I can't tell you."

"Well, he didn't get that from us," Christine said, sounding relieved to be on firm ground. "The quarterly prizes for this year are pocket board games. Here," she bent down and pulled a cardboard box out from under the desk. Inside were several smaller boxes. Hettie saw The Dice Game, Bang, and Star Realm. "If we're lucky we can get a discount for buying several of the same at a time."

"I see." Hettie pulled out her phone and quickly took a photo, not trusting her memory as the games meant nothing to her. They didn't look like twenty-five dollars' worth, but she could check that. She took a chance with her next question.

"But it is true, isn't it, that you've had a complaint about a prize recently?"

"Well, yes. That's what I thought you were here about. This kid, it was a boy, was really upset. I explained that all he'd done was enter a competition, but he said he'd been cheated, and he wouldn't be doing it anymore."

Hettie's interest sparked. "That's what he said? He wouldn't be doing it anymore?"

"Something like that. Kids expect to get something in return for everything they do nowadays."

"Can you remember anything else he said?"

"Well, he was upset, and he said quite a lot, I can tell you. He went on a bit about what he'd supplied being worth a lot more than one of these cars. I told him in the end that he must have called the wrong number."

"That does sound odd," Hettie said. But not if you had a suspicion about what was going on. "Do you ever give money prizes?" she asked.

"We have done, at various times. But I don't mind shopping and wrapping the prizes."

The cost of postage for a small parcel would be higher than for an envelope with a cheque, of course, but considering how much she suspected Christine was saving on the price of the prizes, she was probably skimming quite a bit off the top.

That hadn't been the information she'd come for, but she didn't like what the woman was doing. She was cheating on the newspapers and the children. Mostly the children.

Hettie gave the woman a considered look. "You might want to think about going back to money prizes, just the same," she said. "I don't think these cheap toys are having the effect the newspapers are looking for. Do you?" She watched as the colour rose on Christine's round face. "But thank you for your time. It's been interesting. Come on now, Ceef. Time to go."

Hettie made use of their time on the train

home to do some research on her phone.

"You were right, you know," she told Ceefer. "I wouldn't have gotten that level of information if I'd spoken to Christine Selfridge over the phone."

"Mruff," Ceefer said in agreement.

"And she is most definitely shortchanging the children with those prizes. Those pocket games are worth less than fifteen dollars, nowhere near the twenty-five she's allocated. And a set of six cars, in one-to-sixty-fourth scale, is priced here at just over twenty dollars. That makes each car less than four dollars. Andy received one as a ten-dollar prize." Hettie shook her head. "If I don't see a switch back to monetary prizes very soon, I will be getting in touch with their CEO about this."

"Merrow?"

"Yeah, I know. We need to talk to Stuart about all this too."

Chapter 15

"So, you think the kids involved in this shoplifting gang are receiving payment for what they steal disguised as prizes in Community Newspaper competitions?" Stuart Higgins said. Hettie was sitting in his office at the Rosny Police Station, having told him what she'd just learnt from her visit to the Newspaper offices.

Hettie nodded. "That's why no one has noticed any children suddenly having spending money," she said. "They might even be getting stolen goods as payment in some cases."

"Well, it's as good a theory as any we've come up with, Hettie. We figured it had to be something along those lines, but we hadn't been able to pin it down to anything specific."

"It's simple and very effective," Hettie said. "I expect the children are told to enter the competitions as a means of explaining why they are getting these items. The poor deluded parents are probably pleased to see their children interested in something involving pen and paper and are actually encouraging them."

"You're probably right at that," Stuart said with a wry grin. "I must admit, newspaper competitions weren't something I was ever interested in as a kid. Sooner be out on my bike or kicking a football in the park. This boy Andy, and the girl Ava, give us a starting point. I'll get their details from the school and pay a visit to their parents. Thanks Hettie, good work."

"You're welcome," Hettie said getting up from her seat in front of his desk.

Stuart cleared his throat. "Ah, there is one other thing." Hettie waited. She had a bad feeling about what might be coming next and didn't sit down again. "I've put in a report to headquarters about the circumstances surrounding Roscoe Slater's death. You may get a call about it."

"I see. So you've… escalated it. "

"Mrew."

"There's a discrepancy between the witness statement and your aunt's account of what happened, Hettie. I'm sorry. I can't leave it at that."

"Aunt Alice has never changed her story about what she knows, Stuart. We're not covering up anything. We know as little and as much as the police do."

Except that wasn't entirely true either, was it? They knew what Uncle Roscoe had experienced because his ghost had told Janelle through Aurora. But they knew no more than the police as to what caused the ladder to fall.

"I'm sorry, Hettie. I'm just doing my job."

There was nothing she could say to that. One of the reasons she liked and respected Stuart Higgins was because he was a decent, honest man, and he could do nothing less than carry that attitude into his work. Decent man, decent police officer.

Perhaps it was time for her to speak to Henry Dunlop herself. Just what had he heard when Uncle Roscoe fall off that ladder? She could do that now. They would pass the street where the Dunlops lived on their way home.

They left the police station and headed along the river walkway, crossing over the Cygnet River near Jersey Street. "We're taking a detour here, Ceef," she told him, as they reached the turn into Daisy Street. Her grandfather had been determined to get the name of his best milker in somewhere. "We need to visit the Dunlops."

"Merrooow." Ceefer kept on walking straight ahead.

"I hope you aren't just heading home because you want something to eat," Hettie told him. "I know we're late for lunch but a few more minutes wouldn't hurt."

"MerroOW."

Apparently, they would. Hettie followed him around the corner into Old Dairy Road, past Larry's house, and then Elly's. Hettie was sure Ceefer was heading for home, until he stopped at the edge of the Road and waited for two cyclists to pass. Then he set off across the Road and into the park.

"Ah, I knew this was about food," Hettie told him. "We're just going to the Café aren't we?"

Ceefer didn't even bother to reply to that. He was busy setting a fast pace to his desired destination. Once inside the Café, Hettie unclipped Ceefer's leash but left his harness on. He let out a loud meow at the kitchen door before trotting off toward the laundry where his bowls were kept.

"The master has spoken," Tess giggled, from her spot behind the coffee machine. Her hair was a neon pink today. "Hi, Mrs. P. Your usual?"

"Thanks, Tess." Hettie eyed the muffins and cupcakes in the glass display case but decided to order a salmon and lettuce sandwich to take away. She turned to survey the room. Many of the tables were still occupied with the lunchtime crowd, locals for the most part. The Mrs. B's were absent, but she knew they were having dinner at the Café with Aunt Alice that evening.

Then she noticed the occupants of one of the booths by the side window. Hettie shook her head in wonder. She paid for her topped-up macchiato and carried it to the Dunlop's booth.

"Hello Henry, Lucy," she greeted them. "Could I possibly join you for a few minutes? I'd like to talk to you about something."

"Sure, sure," Henry replied. Lucy slid her short, round body across the seat to make room. Hettie heard a squeak from Lucy's bag, parked on the seat on the far side. She wondered if the little dog inside had been squashed into the corner. The Café staff turned a blind eye to the little fellow, safely tucked away as he was. Lucy patted the bag without looking at it. Guilty conscience.

After inquiring of each other's health and wellbeing, Hettie asked Henry if he remembered the morning Roscoe Slater had died.

"Ah, I feel bad about that," Henry said, jowls wobbling. He had the same body shape as his wife, just a little taller, and larger in the round. "He didn't answer when I called if he were alright, but it weren't unusual for him not to answer, so I didn't give it any thought until the police came asking questions."

"And how is dear Alice?" Lucy asked breathlessly, avid to hear the worst.

"She's doing fine, thank you," Hettie replied, and turned back to Henry. Lucy's faux concern was her annoying method for gathering gossip.

"Henry, Sergeant Higgins said you heard the noise of Roscoe falling and heard him shout out Alice's name."

"That's what it sounded like."

Hettie nodded. "Did you hear anything else around the same time?"

"Like?"

Hettie shook her head. "I don't want to put words in your mouth. I just thought you may have heard some other noises around the same time."

"Like that dog barking, you mean?"

"What dog do you mean?"

"The one that belongs to the woman who's rented your Pearl's place. Big, stupid mutt it is. Howard or something she calls it." Howie may have been a bit dumb, but Hettie preferred him to Lucy's handbag dog. The sight of that skinny rat-like face always made her feel a little queasy.

"So, you heard Howie barking at the time of Uncle Roscoe's accident?"

"Yeah, and her calling out to tell him to be quiet."

"Howie's owner called out?"

"Yeah," Henry nodded, as if Hettie was being particularly dumb, "the woman that's renting the place."

"It couldn't have been a dog in the street you heard barking, could it?"

"Hardly. I've heard that dog bark often enough and heard her shouting at him. It was them alright."

So how did that fit with Lil's story that she was walking Howie when Roscoe fell? It didn't, of course. So what had she seen, or heard, and why had she lied about it?

Hettie chatted to the Dunlops for a few more minutes, asking about their family. Then she thanked Henry for his time and said she would indeed pass on Lucy's best wishes to Aunt Alice.

"I suppose I'll have to thank her when I see her next," Aunt Alice said, when Hettie repeated Lucy Dunlop's condolences later. She had joined her aunt and the Mrs. B's for dinner before her evening games.

"She's a very superficial woman," Mrs. Bronson commented and Mrs. Braxton nodded agreement. Hettie didn't mention anything else about her conversation with the Dunlops. The main topic of conversation in the area lately had been the thunder and lightning show at Aunt Alice's house. Most people believed it had been caused by a malfunction in a piece of video equipment. It was Frank who helped spread that plausible excuse. Hettie felt rather sorry for Gloria because the ghost story she insisted on telling was the true one after all.

Later that evening there was talk among Croquet Club members about the players who were putting their names up for the State Squad. The list Romola had sent to Richie Bolton still only included herself, Jo Isaacs, Tom Eastbourne and Belle Danvers. But it was enough.

They didn't have a date yet for the next coaching session, which would be their first. Hettie had to admit the idea of it was a little daunting but exciting at the same time.

As she was heading for the Café at the end of the evening, Hettie's phone pinged with an email. It was from Isolde Reflex, lawyer and Parke Trust member. She quickly scanned the formally worded epistle, hoping for good news on her request for the extra land for the Club's proposed new courts. She was aware that time was ticking away.

Western Australia was due to host the National Croquet Tournament in eighteen months' time. The event rotated among the six competing states, and what a coup it would be for the Parke Club if they could provide a six-court venue for some of the competitions. Perhaps one of her members could be on the state team by then too.

Unfortunately, it seemed the Trust were still discussing the matter. They wanted to consult with the Bowls Club, only now seeing the need to be even-handed apparently. Ahat had they been doing for the past months since she'd made her formal request? She would have to talk to George Engles again, and soon.

Dan arrived as Violet was closing the Café, so she left the two of them to make their own way and walked home alone with Ceefer. She had something else on her mind that she needed to deal with. Like, who had oiled their backyard gates recently.

It made her uneasy to think someone might be sneaking around their yards at night, although she could see no reason why anyone would. Installing a motion sensitive camera would be one way of finding out what was going on, if anything was, and if the horse hadn't already bolted, so to speak. But she didn't really care for the idea of a spy camera. She'd be aware of it when she was out there herself, and it was an intrusion on privacy.

"I know just the thing, Ceef," she said, as she helped him out of his harness in the hall. "A much simpler way."

She retrieved a reel of black cotton from the sewing box she used for running repairs and went out into her backyard. Starting at the gate to Elly's yard, she broke off a length of thread and attached one end to the fixed part of the gate latch and the other to the latch on the gate itself. She didn't tie it off but simply looped the cotton several times so it would easily pull away unnoticed.

She went to do the same to the gate to Aunt Alice's yard, but as she began to attach the cotton an icy coldness enveloped her hands and arms. She gasped and stepped quickly back. The cold receded immediately, but the brief contact left a lingering sense of anger and sadness.

"U – Uncle Roscoe?" she stammered. She couldn't see anything. Shouldn't there be a sort of shimmering? Something to warn you? She shuddered at the thought of touching him again. "We're – we're doing all we can to find out what happened to you," she whispered. Her heart hammered. "Can – can I get on with this now?"

All was silent. Hettie counted slowly to fifty then took a tentative step forward, one hand in front as if she were feeling her way in the dark. She reached for the latch and completed winding on the cotton, her fingers tripping over one another in their haste.

Back inside and still feeling shivery, she wrapped a shawl around her shoulders and sat at the kitchen table with a hot cocoa. Ceefer jumped up on her lap, rubbing his face against her chin.

"Mrew?"

She smoothed the silky fur on his head. "He was so sad, Ceef. And angry as well. We've got to sort this out somehow, so he can move on."

She woke early as if her mind, eager to check her booby-trapped gates, had set an inner alarm. It was barely light out and the air hadn't warmed up. She pulled on a dressing gown and slipped her feet into the flat shoes she wore about the house. Ceefer was sitting by the back door when she reached it, as if expecting her. But they were to be disappointed. The threads of cotton on the gates were just as she had left them the night before.

"We'll just do it again tonight," she told Ceefer. And every night as often as she needed until she had set her mind at rest, or something was revealed.

Chapter 16

Hettie felt a strong sense of deja vu when she opened her front door later that morning and found Grayson Fox on her doorstep.

"Grayson," she said by way of greeting.

She hadn't seen or heard from him since seeing his car drawing away from in front of her house as she'd left Uncle Roscoe's birthday party not so long ago. He'd obviously called in, found her not at home and hadn't been back since. Had it been a spur of the moment visit that he'd had second thoughts about since?

Without asking she would never know and ask she never would. She had put him out of her mind in any case…up to a point.

"I'd like a word. May I come in?" he asked. Hettie stepped back, closing the door behind him as he headed across the living room and into the kitchen.

She followed, switching on the coffeemaker and reaching for the mugs as if on autopilot. Was this a personal visit or police business? She let him bring up the subject as she watched the coffeemaker.

"We received a request to look into a death that occurred here several weeks back. Roscoe Slater, your aunt's husband I understand."

"Sergeant Higgins called you in did he?"

"Not directly," Grayson said. "The request was passed up the line to homicide and I was asked to deal with it because I already know the people concerned."

Hettie snorted and shot him a look. "Insider information a bonus this time, is it?"

"Don't make this any harder than it needs to be, Hettie," he said taking the mug of coffee she handed him and sitting down at the table. Hettie wished she could forget the times in the distant past when he had sat there. There was something way too familiar about his presence.

"Sit down," he told her when she stood leaning against the kitchen counter. She sighed and sat.

"How much has Stuart told you?" she asked.

"Everything he knows."

"And also, what he suspects, no doubt."

"I'm not getting into a discussion about ghosts, Hettie, but some information doesn't quite gel."

"Doesn't it?" She knew there was a discrepancy too, but she wasn't about to admit it.

"It concerns when a dog barked."

Hettie almost laughed. "Is this like the dog that didn't bark in the night?"

"It wouldn't be the first time a witness didn't want to get involved."

So the police thought Lil had seen what happened but claimed she was out walking Howie, the dog who had barked. The silence lengthened as they sipped their coffee.

"Do you know where I might find your aunt?" Grayson asked. "She wasn't answering her door."

Hettie shook her head. "Not at this moment," she said. No way was she sending him to Elly's place. She wasn't about to tell him Aunt Alice was staying with her either. He might decide to wait for her to return. Her stomach churned. Was he planning to arrest Aunt Alice? His next words didn't make her feel better.

"I would suggest that when you see her, you convince her it's time to tell the truth," Grayson said. "It would save the family a lot of trouble." He got to his feet and put his cup on the drainer. "Please let her know that I'll see her at her home tomorrow morning, around ten. Thanks for the coffee."

Hettie stayed where she was and let him see himself out. She stared unseeing out across the park. So that was how it stood.

"What do you think I should tell him?" Aunt Alice asked over dinner that evening.

"The truth, of course, Auntie. Like Jack said. Just stick to what you've already told them."

Aunt Alice just nodded, but a while later she announced she was going back home.

"I feel Roscoe is lonely there by himself."

"Are you sure you'll be safe?" Hettie wanted to know.

"I think so dear. And I'd feel better being there. I've had a thought too. I'm going to ask Roscoe to make his presence felt when that detective comes calling tomorrow."

Hettie looked at her in alarm. "Ah, I'm not sure that's wise."

"Wise, smise," Aunt Alice said with a dismissive wave. "They don't believe Roscoe is still here. We're never going to convince them unless they see it with their own eyes."

What Hettie was afraid of seeing with her own eyes was Aunt Alice in a jail cell before the week was over.

<><><>

When Hettie went out to check the backyard gates again early Friday morning, she found the cotton hanging off the fixed part of the latch on the gate to Elly's yard. Excited, she raced across to the fence on the other side. There was no cotton at all on the gate to Aunt Alice's yard. She couldn't see it anywhere on the ground either. Someone had passed through both gates during the night. What now? She was gathering pieces of evidence, but she wasn't sure what they meant. Or if their intruder had anything at all to do with Uncle Roscoe's death.

Before she could give the matter more thought, she was called in to take a Sixth-Grade class for the day at Joondalup Primary. She checked in on Aunt Alice before she left.

"Come in dear," Aunt Alice said, holding the front door wide.

"Is it safe?" Hettie asked, stepping tentatively into the hallway.

"I think Roscoe and I have come to an understanding," Aunt Alice confided.

There was a screeching sound close by, and Hettie jumped as the iron umbrella stand bumped her leg, her hand going to her chest.

"Roscoe, not now," Aunt Alice scolded. "You're frightening Hettie."

The umbrella stand screeched back across the floor to its place against the wall. Hettie could feel her heart pounding against her hand. She swallowed.

"Right, um, please be careful, Auntie. When Grayson calls in, I mean. You could get arrested for assaulting a police officer."

Aunt Alice looked shocked. "I won't lay a hand on him, Hettie."

"Of course not, but I don't believe the police have started arresting ghosts. Perhaps you should call Pop. Have him get a lawyer..." A crash from the direction of the kitchen cut off her words.

"You'd better go, Hettie. Apparently, it's quite easy to throw things when you don't need to worry about where they land but moving things with precision takes practice. I think he's finding it rather exhilarating," she confided. "He hasn't had this much life in him since we moved here."

Well, that was a change. Aunt Alice now seemed to be enjoying Uncle Roscoe's presence. Was his ghost about to become a permanent fixture in Old Dairy Road?

Hettie felt uneasy all morning. At lunchtime she tried ringing Aunt Alice to check on her, but there was no answer. She rang Elly, but she hadn't seen her aunt all morning, and according to Violet, Aunt Alice hadn't been to the Café either. Had she been arrested on suspicion of causing Uncle Roscoe's death, or because of something his ghost had done? As a last resort Hettie rang her father.

"Hettie, what's happening?"

"Hi Pop. I'm just checking up on Aunt Alice but she's not answering her phone, and no one seems to have seen her today. Have you heard from her?"

"She rang me this morning. If you want an update on her interview with that Detective Fox, I'm afraid I must disappoint you. He's tied up with some other project and can't see her today after all."

"Oh, that's a relief. Well, for the moment anyway. Are you going to get involved?"

"Don't see the need, Hettie. Not until the police decide to arrest her, anyway, and I can't see that happening. But why Alice thought I'd force her into the Nursing Home I can't imagine."

Hettie was pretty certain that was because she'd threatened Aunt Alice with it and mentally winced. She knew her aunt had told Jack about the police interest, but not sure she had mentioned her husband's ghost. She may not have. Jack might be more amenable to the idea of the Nursing Home if he knew his sister was claiming to see Roscoe in her house.

"Did Aunt Alice say what she was going to be doing today then?" Hettie asked instead.

"She mentioned something about going to a movie with a neighbour," Jack replied.

"Oh, that's nice. What time did she ring?"

"Just before lunch."

There was no cinema in Woody Lake or Rosny, the closest being The Grande in Joondalup. If Aunt Alice spoke to Jack around lunchtime it meant she and Lil would be seeing a two o'clock matinee and not be home before five. She could make use of that. But more importantly, it meant Aunt Alice hadn't been arrested, nor was she lying hurt and unable to call for help because Uncle Roscoe's ghostly pranks had gone awry.

"So what are you planning to do?" Frank wanted to know when Hettie had filled him in on the latest news.

"I need to find out if there's a way from Lil's backyard into Aunt Alice's. I know Max was supposed to remove the gate in the side fence but perhaps someone is climbing over. Perhaps there's a loose panel further down the yard."

"Why would anyone be doing that?" Frank asked.

"I have no idea, Frank, but someone has oiled our gate hinges, and it wasn't Rafe or Larry, or our Mick. And someone is going through our yards at night. I'm wondering if it has something to do with Uncle Roscoe's accident." Unless it was just Alice walking around at night, but Hettie knew she hadn't oiled the gate hinges.

"But Roscoe's accident happened in broad daylight," Frank reminded her. "I can't see the connection."

Hettie huffed. "I can't either but there's something odd going on and I need to figure out what it is."

"Have you heard back from that exorcist yet?"

"No. Not a word. I'm beginning to think Uncle Roscoe's ghost is going to become a permanent addition to the family."

"Look Hettie, don't go doing anything rash tonight, okay? I'd come with you but I'm umpiring an after-school football match today. Can't it wait a few days?"

"I'm going to be looking at a fence, Frank. What could possibly be dangerous about that?"

<><><>

Hettie raced home from school as soon as class was out and headed straight for Aunt

Alice's backyard. This whole thing only made sense to Hettie if it was Lil who was walking through their backyards, and then only if she had some simple way of getting into Aunt Alice's yard.

When Pearl and Max had moved out of Number 10, Larry, as their estate agent, had advised them to remove the gate in their fence that gave direct access to Aunt Alice's yard. Honey myrtles now bloomed on either side of the fence where the gate had once been.

Hettie now made her way to Aunt Alice's back door and knocked, just in case her aunt's plans had changed, and she and Lil hadn't gone out after all. There was no response, except she thought she heard a low rumble inside. If that was Uncle Roscoe, she hoped he would stay where he was. All else was quiet. Lil must have locked Howie inside her house, as Aunt Alice said she did when she went out now.

She surveyed her aunt's yard. All their fences were metal, the regulation six-foot tall with a capping over the sharp top edge. They wouldn't be difficult to clamber over for someone reasonably fit, although the shrubs and trees planted all the way around would make it uncomfortable.

Using a ladder could work too, but either method would show evidence of broken branches, and dents or scratches on the metal fence. It also wouldn't be easy to do quietly. Hardly worth oiling gates if you then made noise clambering over a fence. If it was Lil who was using their backyards as a thoroughfare, she must have some other way of getting into Aunt Alice's yard.

Hettie went down to the far corner. If someone was climbing the fence it would make more sense to do it furthest from the house, where there would be less chance of being heard.. Pushing aside some branches she peered into the shadows. The garden bed was a good three-foot-deep and the dark green paint on the fence made the planting look even denser.

She wriggled her way in trying to avoid getting scratched on the twiggy bits. Above her head, she could see the plantings on Lil's side were just as dense. She ran her hand along the fence, feeling her way over the symmetrically ridged metal and peering at the surface for dents and scratches. She didn't find any, and there didn't seem to be any broken branches in this section either.

Edging back out and rubbing at the scratches on her arms, she decided there had to be an easier way of doing this. She pulled her phone from her pants pocket and turned on the light. Peering in, she ran the light over the fence, covering as far along as she could see clearly. This was much more efficient. She moved along twice more, performing the same task on the next section of fence.

Nothing. There was no evidence of anyone climbing from Lil's yard into Aunt Alice's yard. Was Aunt Alice sleepwalking through their yards at night? Was someone secretly visiting her? None of it made sense. She'd reached the spot where the gate used to be and flashed the phone torch again. There was a small shadow of something.

Chapter 17

Running her fingers along the metal fence, Hettie found a rectangular lump at the spot she had seen the shadow in her torch light. There was a matching one further down. Once a silver colour, they'd been painted green to blend in with the fence panels. They were hinges. What were they doing there if the gate had been removed?

She maneuvered sideways to search for the gate latch and found a sturdy square metal post, also painted green, buried into the ground and reaching the top of the fence. On the other side of the post her fingers found the latch. The gate was still there, but the post prevented it from opening inward.

Lifting the latch and pushing on the gate met with solid resistance. There must be a post on the other side as well. Apparently, Max had rendered the gate inoperable rather than removing it altogether. Not something Larry, or anyone else, seemed to have been aware of. Or perhaps Larry did know and considered it a suitable solution. Hettie couldn't argue with that, but it didn't solve her problem.

She clambered out of the garden and went to the shed for a ladder. She chose the short one with four steps, and not the tall one Uncle Roscoe had been using. She humped it back to the garden. After wrangling the ladder through the branches, and untangling her hair from a persistent twig, she finally got it propped it up against the fence.

A few quick steps up and she'd found the matching post on Lil's side of the fence. She leaned further, putting her hand on it as she peered into the garden. The post moved a little under her hand. That was interesting. The post on Aunt Alice's side was solidly in the ground.

Hettie gripped the top of the fence with both hands, swinging one leg over and then the other. It was a short drop into Lil's yard. Hardly a drop at all, considering the fence was only five inches taller than her, but she'd managed to get a scratch on the back of her neck from a tree branch in the process.

She hunched down and brushed leaves away at the base of the post. Well, that was even more interesting. It was inserted into a round pipe that was sunk into the ground. A square peg in a round hole. A bit of a cliché, that. She grabbed the post in both hands and pulled. It came out easily.

But the gate could only open several inches before it hit a timber planter box that was around the base of the honey myrtle. The opening was nowhere near large enough for anything except a rat to get through. Even without the planter box, the honey myrtle would still be in the way. Why have a post that could be removed if the gate still couldn't open? Had Lil or someone re-jigged the post and then discovered that the tree was in the way. Could someone be that stupid?

Hettie looked around Lil's yard. There were planter boxes around several other trees and shrubs as well. Perhaps they were there to stop Howie digging and damaging the plantings. The boxes must be hinged or something. The planter around the honey myrtle seemed to be full of dead leaves.

Hettie knew from Rafe that it wasn't healthy for a tree to have leaves or soil piled around its trunk, especially when the material got wet. The trunk would rot, and the tree die. Hardly worthwhile putting in the boxes to protect the plants from Howie if you then let them fill up with rubbish.

She wandered along the fence, peering and poking here and there. She could see no evidence of anyone climbing over from this side either. Her wonderful idea had been a dead loss. Feeling completely baffled, she made her back up the fence line to the gate. Picking up the post she put it back in its pipe in the ground.

Reaching up to grab the top of the fence, she put one foot on the edge of the planter box for a boost. As she launched herself, the planter moved under her foot. Her chin hit the top of the fence and pain shot through her jaw. She landed back on her feet, sagging at the knees and supported by her hands still on the top of the fence. She'd bitten her tongue.

Leaning her forehead against the fence, she let her body relax and settle from the shock of the impact. Eventually she braved a look at the planter. Had it collapsed under her weight? She didn't want to leave evidence that someone had been there. Fortunately, it seemed to be in one piece still, but... had it moved?

Hettie was down on her knees in a flash, scraping leaves and soil from the space the planter had uncovered. She found a hard surface. She brushed some more and found an edge. A concrete paver painted brown. Her hands went to the planter box. It wasn't full of dead leaves at all. The honey myrtle was in a square pot inside the box, and the box was on wheels.

Hettie shoved the box sideways and toward the edge of the garden. Jumping to her feet, she pulled the post out again and opened the gate far enough to get through. She could see now that the honey myrtle on Aunt Alice's side had been trimmed at the back, so there was some space between it and the fence.

You would still have to wriggle out between the foliage, but it was possible to come and go through the gate without too much trouble. Mystery solved. She had to admire the ingenuity.

Pulling out her phone, she snapped photos of the open gate, the post lying by the in-ground pipe, and the movable planter. When she was done, she closed the gate and dragged the planter box back to where it had been, piling dead leaves and soil around it to cover the paver.

As she picked up the post, she heard a door opening, followed by a loud bark. She turned, as an excited bundle of fur barrelled into her, knocking her back against the fence.

"What the hell are you doing there?"

Hettie, half hidden behind the honey myrtle, peered out at the woman, whose face radiated suspicion as she looked between her and the square post lying on the ground.

"Uh, hi Lil." Hettie winced. Her face hurt

to speak, and her tongue was painful and thick in her mouth.

Howie put his paws on her waist, pinning her against the fence. He really was a big dog. Thank goodness he was friendly. Unless a command from Lil could change that.

"Well, what are you doing in my yard?" Hettie sensed Lil was unsure how to react, perhaps wondering how much she knew.

She lifted one of Howies' paws off her waist. He took the hint and dropped down on all fours, as if he had lost interest.

"Good boy," she told him, giving the dog a pat on the head. He wandered off. Not the brightest mutt, as Henry Dunlop had said, thank goodness. She pushed a thin branch aside and stepped out of the garden.

"I was just doing some gardening..." she began, wondering where she could go with this. A low rumble came from the other side of the fence. Inspiration struck. "I was pruning the trees and dropped some cuttings on your side of the fence. Uncle Roscoe hated people dropping cuttings back in his yard, and I couldn't do it to anyone either, so I had to come over and collect them." She put her hand to her face. "I banged my chin on the fence and bit my tongue as I was about to climb back."

"You expect me to believe that?" Lil said,

clearly unsure whether to believe her or not.

"It's true. My jaw really hurts," Hettie said deliberately misunderstanding. "I need to take something for it." She stepped back into the garden and reached for the top of the fence.

"I don't think so," Lil said, launching herself at Hettie and pulling her back. Howie barked.

"Lil, for goodness' sake. What is the matter?"

"You've been snooping."

"Why would I be doing that?" Hettie asked, trying to maintain an air of injured innocence. "Please let go of my arm. You're hurting me."

A loud rumble sounded from the other side of the fence and a metal bucket came flying over, just missing them.

"Who's there?" Lil called letting go of Hettie and stepping away. "Alice, is that you?"

"It's Uncle Roscoe," Hettie told her.

"What?" Lil looked around wildly. A patio chair flew over the fence, followed by another. Lil backed further away as Howie barked, leaping around her.

"I'll call the police if you keep this up," Lil threatened, clearly shaken.

"You do that, Lil. I'm sure they'd be interested to hear how you knocked Uncle

Roscoe off his ladder," Hettie said, keeping close to the fence and out of the way of flying objects.

A clap of thunder sounded above their heads. Lil looked up at the clear blue sky, her eyes wide.

"Remember that thunder and lightning show we had recently, Lil? That was Uncle Roscoe." Another clap of thunder, and a shower of small white pebbles rained down on Lil's yard. She ducked, holding her hands over her head as Howie yelped and ran for the back door. "I don't know what he might do, Lil. He's very angry at what you did."

Lil's face was white as a sheet. "I didn't do anything, I wouldn't... I wouldn't hurt anyone. It was Howie." The dog barked again at the sound of his name.

"How could Howie do it, Lil? Did he open the gate by himself?"

Lil groaned. "One of Alice's cats got in and Howie chased it back. He must have bumped the ladder. I heard Roscoe fall, heard him call out. I went and checked on him. There was ... he was... I'm so dreadfully sorry." Whatever else she was guilty of, Hettie found herself believing Lil on this, up to a point.

"So, then you took Howie off for a walk and left Aunt Alice to find Uncle Roscoe. Left her to be suspected of pushing the ladder and killing him."

"It was never meant to be like this," Lil said. "I don't go about hurting people." But using children was acceptable apparently, if what Hettie suspected was true.

"You must have left the gate open," Hettie said.

Lil was quick with a comeback. "The latch must have failed," Not her fault, in other words.

"I guess the post did too."

Lil stared at her for moment, then turned and ran for her back door. Hettie took the opportunity to scramble over the fence. Her feet found the ladder and she all but fell into Aunt Alice's backyard. Her hands shook as she pulled out her phone and called Stuart Higgins, half afraid Lil might decide to come after her.

"Uncle Roscoe?" Hettie queried softly when she'd finished the call and Stuart was on his way. "Are you still here?" The answer came in a low rumble close beside her and she jumped. "Oh, um, Aunt Alice should be home soon. I guess you know what happened now." Another rumble. "Good, well, that's good, isn't it? I hope everything works out for you, I really…"

Chilly air surrounded her, and she gasped.

The coolness lasted only several seconds before she was left with a feeling of warmth that was more than just physical. She had the distinct feeling she'd just been hugged by a ghost.

Chapter 18

Stuart Higgins called in a few days later to give them the latest news. The family were sitting in Hettie's living room once again. Stuart accepted a beer from Larry and took a mouthful. They knew from news reports that Lil had been arrested, and the shoplifting operation put to an end.

"So, she really was using our backyards as a secret passage?" Gwen asked.

"Yes," Stuart replied, "her couriers would leave a backpack of goods at your gate to the side street, collect an empty backpack she'd left out, and go on their way. She didn't show herself to the couriers at all. Then she simply carried the stuff through your backyards to her own place. Our stakeout on Sunday night caught two of the couriers, young fellows on bikes."

"I wonder if it was Howie who discovered the gate. She must have been pleased to find a secret passage that kept her operation away from her own front door," Hettie said.

Stuart nodded. "It certainly added an extra level of cover for her operation."

"And an extra chance of something going wrong," Gwen said. "Which it did."

"What about the children who were shoplifting?" Elly asked. "What will happen to them?"

"Those we know of have been spoken to and warned. I expect their parents will be keeping a close eye on them for some time."

"It's scary, knowing how easy it must have been to get them involved," she said, clearly finding that a worry.

"It takes a village to raise a child," Aunt Alice said. "You have that, Elly."

Elly smiled. "Thanks, Auntie. I don't know what I'd do without your help."

"I'd like to know how she was disposing of all these shoplifted items," Larry said. "If she was doing it on the internet, surely they could be traced?"

"That was one of the things that made it difficult to uncover," Stuart said. "She hadn't sold anything yet. We think she was going to run the operation until we started to close in, and then she would disappear with her haul, and start selling it off from a different location, under a different name, and by whatever methods of disposal she could find. It isn't the first time she's done this, apparently. We found forged driver's licences and other identity documents. She'd already run her programme in several cities in Queensland. I suspect we may find links to other places as well."

"What a waste," Gwen said. "If she were that clever, she could have done almost anything."

"She could certainly play the part of a good neighbour, anyway," Hettie said.

"Talking of neighbours, you took a risk going into Lil's yard on your own, Hettie," Gwen told her. "Why didn't you call me? I would have come and helped." She was clearly put out that she hadn't been included.

"I didn't think there was a risk," Hettie argued. "I thought Lil was out with Aunt Alice at the movies. I didn't know the neighbour she'd spoken of to Pop was actually Mrs. Bronson."

"One could argue Mrs. Bronson isn't exactly a neighbour," Gwen suggested. "It was misleading, at least."

"A neighbour isn't just someone who lives right next door, Gwen," Aunt Alice retorted. "It's people who live in the neighbourhood. Ila just lives a little further along the Road."

Hettie held up her hands. "We are not going to argue about semantics. I made an assumption, and it was wrong. But just think. If I hadn't, we'd be sitting here tonight still worrying about what was going on and what to do about Uncle Roscoe's ghost. Instead, we're celebrating."

"Cheers to that," Larry said. Glasses were raised in agreement.

"I hadn't expected to be hearing anything more about ghosts," Stuart said, looking around at everyone. Hettie was sure he expected to see embarrassment on their faces, but they all met his gaze. Perhaps now he thought they were just brazen.

"Roscoe's moved on," Aunt Alice told him. "He only wanted to know who had knocked over the ladder. We don't understand everything."

"We even have a cat who knows more than he should," Larry added.

"Mruff," Ceefer agreed as if he'd understood what Larry had said. Which, of course, he had. That response set Stuart back a bit, Hettie was amused to see.

"I have an announcement to make," Callie said, looking more than a little pleased with herself. The family members sitting around the table in the Sunny Vale Community Centre dining room that Sunday looked at her expectantly.

"I knew it," Gloria said. "You've finally come to your senses and realised I'm right about those government drones spying on us."

Eddie patted Gloria's arm and urged her to be quiet and listen. Gloria shook her head, dark curls slipping from her hair clip, but didn't say anything more.

Callie ignored the interruption. "Next month," she announced, "I'm hosting a charity auction here in the Community Centre. I expect you all to attend and I'm expecting each one of you to supply at least one worthy donation to be auctioned off. It can be something you already have, or it can be a service you can perform, or you can solicit a donation from someone else. But I want this to be a great success and raise a lot of funds for our cause."

Hettie immediately thought of buying several year-long memberships to the Bowls Club to auction off. New members might sweeten George's attitude to her plans for the Croquet Club.

"What is this charity auction in aid of, California," Aunt Alice asked.

"So glad you asked, Alice." Callie took a deep breath. "It's for a very worthy cause.

Something close to my heart we can all be very proud of. The establishment of the new Parke Museum."

Hettie imagined you could have heard a pin drop. Even little Rosa stopped gabbling. Hettie glanced at her father. It was clearly the first he'd heard of this very worthy cause. He cleared his throat.

"There, ah, there might be some discussion yet as to where the funds from this auction are to be directed," he said. "A final decision has yet to be made." Which from Callie's expression was not what she expected or wanted to hear. But what on earth had she been thinking? A Parke Museum? What had she been planning to display? Her family?

"Perhaps we could come up with some suggestions, sir," Rafe offered.

"Capital idea, Rafe," Jack said, grabbing at the thought. "If enough money is raised, we could even spread it among several worthy causes. I suggest they be limited to Woody Lake and Rosny. Let's keep it local."

"A charity auction is a wonderful idea, California," Alice told her. "I'm sure you can turn it into a classy event that will be remembered for years. Just as soon as some rather important details are worked out."

"Thank you, Alice," Callie said, seeming to

take only the positive from the comment. Jack patted her hand, and she smiled as discussions broke out around the table on how and where the monies could be used.

"Did you know about this museum nonsense?" Hettie asked Pearl as they were leaving the dining room.

"No, absolutely not. I knew Mum was planning the auction, but I'd been sworn to secrecy."

"How in heaven did she imagine anyone would be interested in a Parke Museum? People would've stayed away in droves."

Pearl nodded in agreement. "I suspect it's not the first madcap idea Pop's had to reign in over the years."

"Oh, gosh, you don't think she has more in common with Gloria, do you? Is there a mad Garcia gene we might have inherited?"

"What's this about mad Garcias?" Frank wanted to know from behind them.

"We were just wondering if Callie had more in common with Gloria than we realised," Hettie said turning to him.

"Oh, lord, isn't one enough? It is possible though," he said considering. "Though it might have come from our grandfather's mother, and not from a Garcia at all, if the stories Dad tells me are anything to go by."

"But it's the Garcia line it's being passed down on," Hettie pointed out.

Her phone pinged with an incoming email. It was the response to her application to the exorcist, requesting more details. She quickly emailed back. "Thank you, but the problem has been resolved."

Looking up from her phone she found Larry and Max had joined them. She'd noticed that Max hadn't seemed his usual jovial self today, but how could he have even imagined that not removing the gate would result in a death. He'd done what he thought was needed to secure it. It was all rather sad.

"Everyone's invited back to our place for drinks," Larry announced. "We need to decide on some worthy causes that need money, and make sure this charity auction is a success."

Just what they needed after the past months, Hettie thought, as they made their way down the park. Something positive to look forward to.

* * * * * *

Your Free Read

HAVE YOU got your free copy of *Miranda's Last Case?* In this story you will not only discover how Ceefer came to live in Woody Lake with Hettie and Violet, but you will also meet Miranda Black. Miranda, a retired British agent, will be starring in her own series, Miranda's Case Books to be introduced in 2026. Download *Miranda's Last Case* here, and we will keep in touch so you can learn more about us and our writing.

Next in Series

Death by Candlelight

Hettie Parke is at her wit's end. Her mother's attempt to link the Parke name with something positive sadly fails when someone trips over the body of property developer Carl Dalrymple at her charity auction in the Sunny Vale Community Centre. And has Hettie heard her correctly? Does Callie really want her to investigate this death?

With the murder linked to a claim that her grandfather's land was acquired by fraud, it's hardly a surprise when the police investigation led by that detective considers her family likely suspects. But Hettie is frustrated and upset when her investigation goes astray and her overly enthusiastic group of elderly sleuths find themselves in danger. So when someone else's life comes under threat it's Ceefer whom Hettie calls on for help.

Can they prevent another death and unmask the killer, or will some suspicions continue to remain a mystery?

About the Author

Irene Sauman writes historical cozy mysteries. Under her pen name, Rennae Todd, she has written cozy mysteries in a present-day setting. Irene is a retired historian who grew up on a vineyard and orange orchard by the Murray River in New South Wales. She was an avid reader and started writing stories when she was nine years old (including some quite dreadful poetry).

Now living in Western Australia, she has three children and four grandchildren, and a sister who beta reads her books for plot holes and to see how quickly she can solve the mystery.

When not writing (or reading), Irene watches tennis, plays croquet, and has a reasonably green thumb, which means very little dies in her garden, unlike in her cozy mysteries.

Irene and Rennae share a website irenesaumanauthor.com where you can learn more about their books which are available in ebook and print, and from online libraries.

Follow us on BookBub for new releases

Irene's BookBub page

Rennae's BookBub page

Our Books

Murray Valley Mysteries
by Irene Sauman

This series of four cozy historical mysteries is set in the eighteen-seventies on the Murray River where Emma Haythorne's comfortable life at Wirramilla, her family's sheep station, is about to be turned upside down. There's a murder, and an old promise raises its ugly head. She might be able to solve the murder, but what she does to avoid the promise leaves her with a share in a riverboat and a business partner who doesn't approve of anything she does, especially getting involved in murder. Would she have fared better if she'd honoured the promise?

Find out starting with Book #1 *Saddled with Death* or download the box set and read the complete series.

Victorian Country Town Mysteries
by Irene Sauman

Read on from the Murray Valley Mysteries and follow Emma's life into a new decade.

It's 1884. Emma is settling into a new life in the country town of Echuca, the main port on the Murray River. She is thankful to have Janey and Abe for help and company, but she's not sure what to do with herself.

But where Emma is concerned murder is never far away and once she gets involved with one, others follow. She soon has more than enough to fill her time as fellow residents prove interested in her herbal remedies, despite there being doctors in town, and there's also the Ladies Benevolent Society, providing they don't object to a member sullying her hands with suspicious deaths on occasion. Sergeant Donovan may one day even approve of her, though possibly not the coroner, Dr. MacArthur.

Join Emma in her new life. *Death in Disguise* is the first title in the series.

Miranda's Case Books
by Irene Sauman

Miranda Black, 62-year-old former British agent for the Department, is seeking a peaceful and uneventful retirement. Point Placid, a characterful seaside town on the west coast of Australia is just what she needs. Until she finds the body of the local historian on the beach, drawn to the scene by the cries of a black cat.

Amid the stories of smuggling past and present, a proposed development that has divided the town, and families who don't want their nefarious past brought to light Miranda can't help but become involved. After all she's used to getting things done outside of normal channels. And while the police aren't so keen on that approach Miranda's equally elderly neighbour and her outspoken and bolshie niece are keen to assist and advise.

Can Miranda help solve a murder while still finding her place in her new hometown? Or will Point Placid be her undoing? This series is coming in 2026 with the first title *Murder at the Lighthouse*.

Murray Valley Mysteries
Saddled with Death
A Gem of a Problem
A Body in the Woodpile
Murder at the Mill
Murray Valley Mysteries 1-4

Victorian Country Town Mysteries
Death in Disguise
Death of a Lady (2026)

Woody Lake Mysteries
Malice Aforecourt
Betwixt and Bewitched
A Christmas in July Sundowner Sally
Death by Candlelight
Grave Double
Woody Lake Mysteries 1-4

Miranda's Case Books
Murder at the Lighthouse (2026)
Murder in the Paint